Sadie would be a good mommy for Ellie. There was no denying it.

Cam watched as Sadie pointed to one of the monkeys in the far right corner picking bugs from its head and eating them. Ellie's laugh filled the air.

Though part of him felt sadness for Ellie's quick acceptance of Sadie, the other part of him praised God for it. With Cam's feelings growing each passing day, it made the possibility of dating Sadie much easier to consider.

He'd felt such peace at the cemetery about being able to let Brenda go. Maybe this was God's sign that Ellie would be ready, too.

JENNIFER JOHNSON and her unbelievably supportive husband, Albert, are happily married and raising Brooke, Hayley, and Allie, the three cutest young ladies on the planet. Besides being a middle school teacher, Jennifer loves to read, write, and chauffeur her girls. She is a member of American Christian Fiction Writers. Blessed beyond measure, Jennifer hopes to always think like a child—bigger than imaginable and with complete faith. Send her a note at jenwrites4god@bellsouth.net.

Books by Jennifer Johnson

HEARTSONG PRESENTS
HP725—By His Hand
HP738—Picket Fence Pursuit
HP766—Pursuing the Goal
HP802—In Pursuit of Peace

Finding Home

Jennifer Johnson

Heartsong Presents

This book is dedicated to my little sister, Tabitha Lydia Miles. Tabitha, you are a truly beautiful young lady, not only physically, but also because of your deep love for Jesus. I pray that God blesses your life and that you always strive to live for Him. I love you.

A note from the Author:
I love to hear from my readers! You may correspond with me by writing:

Jennifer Johnson
Author Relations
PO Box 721
Uhrichsville, OH 44683

ISBN 978-1-60260-560-2

FINDING HOME

Scripture taken from the HOLY BIBLE, NEW INTERNATIONAL VERSION®. NIV®. Copyright © 1973, 1978, 1984 by International Bible Society. Used by permission of Zondervan. All rights reserved.

All of the characters and events in this book are fictitious. Any resemblance to actual persons, living or dead, or to actual events is purely coincidental.

Our mission is to publish and distribute inspirational products offering exceptional value and biblical encouragement to the masses.

PRINTED IN THE U.S.A.

prologue

The unrelenting wails of the newborn filled the hospital delivery room. All other noise—beeps of monitors, instructions from the doctor, murmurs from nurses—seemed to stop. Sadie could only hear the cries of the infant. Before her mind could wrap around the truth of what had just happened, the doctor laid the squalling child on Sadie's chest.

Sadie looked at the babe, barely wiped off from having just made her entrance into the world. The tiny girl had a head full of dark brown hair, just like her mama.

But I'm not her mama.

In truth, Sadie had just delivered the baby, but she wouldn't be the child's mother. Brenda Reynolds would be her mom, and Cam Reynolds would be her dad.

Tears filled Sadie's eyes. The six- or seven-pound weight of the baby seemed more than her chest could bear. Sadie's legs shook with no hope of ever stopping. It was as if every emotion she'd ever known in her life had left her body with the delivery of the baby. Now her body remained little more than a cavity, raw and empty.

Touching the baby's soft head ever so slightly with her fingertips, a wave of emotion washed over her as quickly as it had evaporated only moments before. *I love you, baby girl.*

As if sensing Sadie's thoughts, the child quieted and looked up into Sadie's eyes. Her gaze seemed to say, "So you are my mommy." Sadie's heart broke and tears streamed down her cheeks. The moment ended and the tiny girl began another chorus of squalls.

"Would you like to kiss her before she goes?" The nurse's voice was soft, and Sadie noted the tenderness in the older woman's expression.

She nodded and pressed a soft kiss on the infant's head. "I love you, little girl," she whispered before lifting the bundle into the nurse's arms.

The nurse wrapped the baby—Sadie's baby—in a pink blanket and walked out of the room. Sadie knew Cam and Brenda waited outside the door. They waited for their baby, for her baby.

The emptiness, sheer, strong, and painful, overwhelmed her again. A sudden heaving of sobs filled her chest and spilled from a void that made no sense. How could she feel so much in the midst of such emptiness? How could this be happening to her?

There are always consequences for actions.

The reminder wasn't condemnation, but rather a fact. Sadie had chosen to step outside of God's will, and natural consequences had taken place. Having left the safety of her parents' home for college, Sadie had fallen into the arms of her first real love. At least, Sadie thought it had been love. But when Sadie discovered she was pregnant, her boyfriend wanted out of the relationship, and her parents were devastated. At nineteen, Sadie knew she couldn't raise the baby. Her college church family guided her through the adoption process.

And now my baby is gone.

Sobs racked her body again. She knew God had forgiven her sin. She knew God was guiding her life once more. She knew God had led her to the right couple to adopt her baby girl.

So why do I feel so much pain?

one

Five years later

Rain beat Sadie's windshield. The sky, dark and angry, fueled Sadie's mood. The father of one of her students had been undeservedly harsh because his son had not made the progress dear ol' Dad felt was appropriate. As an occupational therapist for their small county in North Carolina, Sadie had shown the man document after document detailing the marked improvements his young son had made since the car accident that had stolen much of the child's memory, including his academic memories. This father wanted his son to be "just like everyone else" and negated the wonderful strides the boy and his special education teacher had made. Paining Sadie further, he'd voiced his complaints in front of the child. Sadie wondered how much harder it would be to help the student improve when the new school year rolled around again.

Frustrated, Sadie parked the car in front of her small apartment. In less than a month, the lease would be up on the one-bedroom place she'd called home for the last two years. The weeks couldn't pass fast enough.

Sadie grabbed the umbrella from the backseat, stuck it out the driver's door, and popped it open. The wind caught it, flipping it inside out and rendering the umbrella useless. Letting out a disgruntled huff, Sadie stepped out of the car and straight into a puddle.

"That's just great," she muttered as she lifted her nearly

new suede shoe out of the puddle. "Okay, this day can only get better."

She swiped a wet strand of hair away from her cheek and raced toward her mailbox. Five years and two weeks had passed. She knew that any day she would receive a package containing several pictures and a letter. Rain, sleet, hail, sunshine—nothing would keep her from checking the mail until that package arrived.

She opened the mailbox door. A large, white, duct-taped envelope rested beneath a pile of junk mail. Gingerly, she pulled it out and noted the Delaware address in the top left-hand corner. *It's here.* She tucked her treasure into her jacket, protecting it from the elements.

She raced to the front door and fumbled with her keys to unlock the door. Her heart raced in anticipation of opening the package. Once inside, she kicked off her shoes and placed the mail on the table. After racing into her bedroom, she slipped into a comfortable gown and a robe. She wanted to relish every picture, devour every word Brenda Reynolds wrote. Being garbed in wet clothes would only distract her.

With shaky hands, she grabbed her "Ellie" album from the bookshelf in her bedroom. How could she ever repay the Reynoldses for naming the baby after her? Five years before, Sadie Ellis had given birth to a baby girl, and her adoptive parents, Cam and Brenda Reynolds, named her Ellie in honor of the birth mother. What other adoptive parents would do that?

Unexpected tears filled her eyes as she thought of how God had blessed her baby with the perfect couple. To this day, this very moment, Sadie wished she had been able to keep her little girl. And yet Sadie knew then, as she still intellectually knew now, God had provided Cam and Brenda for Ellie.

Sadie cuddled up on her couch with the album and package. As she did every year, she looked at the album before she opened the new package. She wanted to reexperience Ellie's growth from year to year and then bask in the changes the new package would reveal.

The first year of Ellie's life, Sadie had been surprised at how much she looked like her biological father. But the next year, Ellie's appearance shifted to look more like Sadie. By the time she was four, Ellie's hair had grown just past her shoulders and her eyes had deepened to a dark brown, the same shade and almond shape as Sadie's.

Finally, it was time to open the mail. Inhaling deeply, Sadie peeled back the tape. Several pictures fell out. Sadie devoured each. One specific picture held Sadie's attention. Ellie sat on the floor with a group of children, probably at preschool, or maybe Sunday school. Ellie sat sideways toward the camera, her focus on a blond girl sitting beside her. Her dark hair fell well past her shoulders, a bit disheveled from a day of play. Long eyelashes framed dark eyes. Her cheeks were a bit pinker than they should have been, and Sadie wondered if Ellie had been wind-kissed only moments before. But her smile. Sadie couldn't take her eyes from the smile that lit Ellie's face. Her little girl was happy, and Sadie was so thankful.

After several minutes, Sadie picked up the single-page letter that had fallen from the package. *That's strange. Brenda usually writes several pages.* After opening the sheet, Sadie realized Brenda hadn't written at all. It was from Cam. She read it quickly.

Hello Sadie,

Ellie has grown a lot this year. I guess you can see that from the pictures. She's a great kid. I wouldn't have known

how to deal with Brenda's death had it not been for Ellie.
I know sometimes it can be hard for her without her mom.
If you ever want to visit Ellie, that would be great. Not the
norm for a regular adoption situation, but hey, who says
what's normal? Just let me know.

Cam Reynolds

Sadie skimmed through the note again. "What?" She
rested her hand on her chest. "Brenda is dead?"

She scooped up each letter from the previous years, scouring
them for any hint as to what happened to Brenda. Had
she been sick? Was she in an accident? What could have
happened? Sadie couldn't find a hint of a reason.

Brenda must have died in an accident. But when? How long
had she been gone? Why wouldn't Cam have told her? *Why*
would Cam have told me? I gave my baby to him. He doesn't
have to tell me anything.

Sudden, full realization weighed on her heart, and she
picked up a picture of Ellie. She traced the child's face with her
finger. Cam was the only parental figure in Ellie's life now. She
remembered him to be a man who worked hard with his hands
but didn't have a lot to say. He was a man who would probably
be a super dad to a bouncing baby boy, but what would he be
like raising a little girl on his own? Tears pooled in her eyes.
Her baby didn't have a mother.

❧

Cam rubbed his biceps before knocking on the babysitter's
door. The days had been almost never-ending the last month,
as he'd finished the remodeling of the older home he'd
found for his sister and her daughters. Her husband, Tim,
had passed away only two months before, and it hadn't been
difficult to talk Kelly into moving herself and the girls back

to Delaware. Finding a reasonably priced house with few renovations needed was another story.

Though Kelly and the girls had been out of Cam's home and into their own the last week, the house still had several small problems to keep him busy. His business renovations had taken a beating due to the time he'd spent at Kelly's. Thankfully, he would be able to focus on his work again beginning the next week.

"Daddy!" Ellie's squeals pierced through the screen door before he'd had a chance to actually knock.

"Come here, Ellie-Bellie." Cam pulled open the door then lifted Ellie up to his chest. She was a bit big to be held in this way, but she was his little girl; she'd be his *only* little girl, and as long as she would let him, he would hold her. With his free hand, he waved at his babysitter. "Thanks so much, Ann. We'll see you later."

The middle-aged woman smiled. "See you Monday, Ellie."

In only a few strides, he reached his truck and slipped Ellie into her seat belt. He made his way around to the driver's side. "So how was your day?"

"Good. What's for dinner, Daddy?" Ellie looked out the window. "We made fish sticks for lunch at Ms. Ann's house. She let me push the sticks in a line. Trudy tried to mess up my rows of sticks, but Ms. Ann told her no. I told her no, too. It isn't nice to mess up people's stuff, is it, Daddy?"

Cam shook his head and inhaled a deep breath. *Oh boy, here we go.* He loved his daughter—adored her more than life itself—but when that child got to talking, a man's head could burst from the incessant chatter.

"And then when it was naptime, you know what that Trudy did? She took my blankie. She knows I have to have my blankie."

Cam nodded and looked at the seat next to Ellie, spying the shredded peach and green material. *Whew. She must have had it in her hand when I picked her up.* Once upon a time, a doll and lamb had been quilted into the piece of fabric, but it had been well over a year since the blanket even remotely resembled what it had once been. Ellie took it with her everywhere. He couldn't even count the times he'd had to drive back to Ann's house to retrieve Ellie's special blanket. With Ellie just turning five, maybe it was time she became less attached to the matted piece of material. But Cam didn't have the heart to take it from her, especially since Brenda had died only ten months ago.

Her death hadn't come as a surprise. He had watched Brenda's valiant battle with breast cancer for two years. He and Ellie, even at her sweet young age, had been prepared that Brenda might need to "go live with Jesus," as Ellie said. Whether they were prepared or not, her death had still been hard. His five-year-old toting a dilapidated old blanket around with her was the least of his concerns.

"And then when it came time for you to come get me, Trudy said. . ."

Cam pulled the truck into the driveway and put it in park. He took in the length of his yard. Already it needed mowed again. He loved spring. Normally, he welcomed the season and the opportunity to dig into the earth of his land. This year, he just didn't have time for yard work.

"Daddy, you never said what we're gonna eat for dinner. I'm hungry, Daddy." She unbuckled her own seat belt and jumped off her booster car seat.

Cam grinned as he grabbed her hand in his. "I think we'll make spaghetti."

"Mmm. I love sgabetti." Ellie's face shone with pleasure.

Yet another thing he hadn't been able to bring himself to correct her about. Ellie often mixed up the pronunciations of large words, but the mix-ups were simply so cute, he didn't have the heart to point them out. He escorted her into the house.

"I'll stir the sauce, and I want to put the sgabetti into the pan. Oh, but I have to go potty first, Daddy. Okay?"

Cam grinned as he laid the keys on the counter. He watched as Ellie rushed down the hall toward the bathroom. "Make sure you wash your hands, Ellie."

"I will, Daddy."

Cam walked into the pantry and took down a can of spaghetti sauce and a box of pasta. If Brenda were still alive, she would have made them homemade sauce, filled with meat, tomatoes, peppers, and onions. Brenda made the best spaghetti sauce around. It was a family favorite when his sister's family and his parents came to visit. Now he and Ellie simply dumped sauce from a can.

His little girl trotted back into the kitchen and pulled a chair up to the counter. After stepping up onto it, she grabbed the sauce, attempting to pop the lid. Pursing her lips, she twisted the lid unsuccessfully until her face turned red.

"Need some help?"

She handed him the can then swiped a chunk of hair away from her eyes. "I can't get it, Daddy."

He popped the lid, and within minutes, Cam and Ellie had fixed their supper. After listening to several more injustices that the infamous Trudy had bestowed upon Ellie, Cam and his daughter finished their supper and put the dishes in the dishwasher, and he gave Ellie a bath.

"Daddy, can Trudy spend the night tomorrow?"

Cam grinned. "We'll see, pun'kin."

Cam brushed Ellie's long dark hair. It was much easier to deal with if he worked out the kinks while it was wet. The girl ended in tears when he tried to comb through tangles once it had dried. He couldn't begin to count the times her babysitter had to fix her hair after he got her to Ann's house.

Once finished, Ellie twirled around in her pink pajamas. "Do I look like a princess, Daddy?"

"The prettiest princess I've ever seen."

Ellie pushed her long strands of hair from her eyes. "Will you tell me a mommy story?"

Cam sucked in a deep breath. He knew she'd ask. She did nearly every night. Tonight he felt raw, raw to his very core. He missed Brenda. Missed her kiss when he walked in the door from work. Her soft touch when he'd had a long day. He'd taken over so many of the household chores during her sickness that he hadn't realized how much he still needed her presence until she was gone.

Cam closed his eyes and blew the air from his chest. "Well, one time, when you were just a tiny baby, I came home from work and Mommy was holding you real close and rocking you in the rocking chair. She was still wearing her pajamas, and so were you."

Cam tickled Ellie's belly, and she giggled. "Her hair was all messy. Dishes and clothes were all over the house. I was worried that you or Mommy were sick."

Ellie's eyes widened; then she frowned. "Mommy was sick, wasn't she?"

Pain sliced through Cam's heart. Ellie had witnessed sickness too much in her young life. He wished he could have protected her from it. "No, pun'kin. She had spent the whole day rocking you. She said she loved you so much she just couldn't put you down."

Ellie smiled. "I love Mommy, too. One day we'll see Mommy in heaven with Jesus."

"Yes, we will."

Ellie wrapped her arms around Cam's neck. "I love you, Daddy." She jumped beneath her covers and cuddled up with her blankie.

"I love you, too." Cam leaned down and kissed her forehead. Thankfully, unlike his sister's girls, Ellie loved bedtime.

Cam turned off her light then walked to his room. After getting ready for bed, he slipped between his king-sized covers and stared at the empty space beside him. *Ten months and four days. Lord, I miss her so much.*

Sadie sipped the coffee she'd brewed herself. The grocery-store French vanilla flavoring proved nowhere near as good as the java she enjoyed from her favorite gourmet coffee shop. But she had spent her budgeted coffee allowance two days before and payday wasn't until tomorrow. Though not a miser, Sadie prided herself on being frugal with her income. Staying faithful to her budget allowed her to save a substantial amount of money to put into a savings account for a down payment on a house. *I'll be a homeowner by the time I'm twenty-five.*

The reminder brought a smile to Sadie's lips. She took another sip, believing the taste to be better than she'd originally thought. Opening her laptop, she pictured the small two-bedroom house she'd viewed online. With its covered porch and neatly manicured lawn, Sadie had instantly fallen in love with the home. *If only I felt as content about living here in this county.*

She turned on the computer. *Lord, Paul learned to be content in all situations. Show me how. Is there a reason I don't like it here?*

Her discontent made no sense. She lived in one of the most beautiful places in the United States, on the edge of the Smoky Mountains in North Carolina. She attended a wonderful church with a booming singles' group. Sadie filled most of her weekends helping her closest friend with her toddler sons. She worked for a terrific school system and for one of the kindest Christian women she'd ever met. And yet something was missing.

She pulled up the Realty Web site and selected the link to the small home. "Sold?" She blinked and peered at the four bright red letters covering the picture. "But it wasn't even under contract yesterday."

Sadie grabbed the phone and dialed the Realtor's number, sure that a mistake had been made. She listened, stunned, as the secretary explained that a client had purchased the home outright the day before.

Saddened to the core, Sadie called her friend Lisa. The phone rang a few times, was answered, and then crashed to the floor. Amazingly, it stayed connected and Sadie could hear the faint murmurs of "Hi. Hi. Hi." A smile bowed Sadie's lips. Without a doubt, one of the boys had answered the phone and was talking into the wrong end. Just as she started to hang up and try again, more rustling sounded over the line and Sadie heard a frantic "Hello?"

"Hey, Lisa. Sounds like the boys have you hopping."

A long sigh sounded. "Don't they always? But hey, I was going to call you later. Guess what?"

"What?"

"Our house sold. Looks like Rick and I will be making the move to Alabama."

Sadie's heart crashed to the bottom of her gut. "But your house has been on the market for two years. I didn't think you were even serious about moving anymore."

"We never stopped praying about it. You know that. Rick's dying to be closer to his family. And I'm still not kidding about you coming with us and getting a job there, and—"

Sadie interrupted her. "I'm not moving to Alabama."

A long sigh sounded again. "I know. And I'm going to miss you something awful."

Doom seemed to wrap itself around Sadie. First, she discovered Brenda had died. Next, her dream house sold out from under her. Now, her only close friend was moving hundreds of miles away. Raw emotion threatened to expose itself. She swallowed and said the first thing she could think of. "My house sold, too."

"Ah, Sadie. I'm sorry."

The genuine sympathy in her friend's tone brought tears to Sadie's eyes. "It's okay. God knows what. . ." She couldn't finish the sentence. She believed God, trusted Him with every fiber of her being. But right now she felt robbed. Gypped. And very much alone.

"Rick has to work tonight. Why don't you come over later? We'll watch a movie together."

"Okay. I'll call you later." A tear streamed down her cheek. Swiping it away, Sadie determined to hold herself together. A breakdown would only make her friend feel worse. "I've got to get to work. I'll call you later."

Before Lisa could respond, Sadie hung up the phone then grabbed a tissue out of its box. Dabbing her eyes, she inhaled several times to keep tears from ruining her makeup before the day even began. She imagined what her life would be like without Lisa. Sure, she participated in several of the singles' outings put together by the church. She'd even gone on a few dates with a couple of guys. But the only person in North

Carolina she'd grown close to was Lisa. Probably because Lisa had helped Sadie get through the loss of Ellie to adoption, and then later allowed Sadie to be the godmother to her precious two-year-old twin boys. Sadie stared back at the screen of her laptop for several moments. The SOLD sign smacked across the picture of the house that Sadie had prayed so fervently for seemed to mock her. *What now, God?*

A sudden idea sped through her, lightening her heart faster than she would have believed. A frivolous thought, really. And yet the impression was so strong, and her curiosity so piqued, Sadie couldn't help but type the words into her favorite search engine. *When nothing is there, I'll know it's just a silly notion.*

Within seconds, the Web site popped up. Sadie selected the Job Vacancies link and scrolled down. *Surely not?* She stared at the opening for several minutes.

Blinking a couple of times, she took a long gulp of her coffee. She looked at the occupational therapist opening in the school district where Cam and Ellie lived. "God, is this merely a strange coincidence?"

She leaned back in her chair. Why had she even considered checking out the site to begin with? She had no business even dreaming of visiting Ellie, let alone living near her. She bit her bottom lip. And yet wasn't it Cam who suggested she visit? Maybe it would be okay to simply send in her application and résumé. Just to see what happened.

But he didn't say I should move near them.

She shook the thought away as her heart fluttered at the idea of seeing Ellie on a regular basis. She'd made poor choices before her pregnancy with Ellie, but since then she'd kept her head about her and sought God in decisions she had to make, both big and small. And in truth, she didn't believe in coincidences. She believed God's hand was in every circumstance of His children, even the hard ones.

"Maybe, God, this is from You?"

two

Cam scratched at the day's growth of stubble on his jaw as he looked over his home renovation business's financial sheet for the month of April. The month had been a rough one, his expenses outweighing his income. Thankfully, he'd thrown himself into his work the first six months after Brenda's death, and his wallet could afford one bad month.

Now that Kelly and the girls are settled into their house, I'm going to have to focus on my business again. He put the sheet on his desk and picked up the stack of work requests. Honest pride filled him as he sifted through potential clients. God had always blessed his hard labor and given him a multitude of customers seeking his skills. Living just over thirty miles from historic Wilmington, Delaware, didn't hurt much either.

He glanced at the clock. Kelly would be expecting him for dinner in a little over an hour. Ellie had spent the day with her aunt and cousins. Kelly's girls were all older than Ellie, but they loved their little cousin and doted on Ellie every chance they could.

Until Kelly moved back to Delaware, Cam didn't realize how thankful he'd be to have her living near him. Their parents had retired to Florida several years before, so he and Ellie only saw them every four to six months. Brenda's parents lived in Nevada, and Ellie hadn't seen them since Brenda's death. They'd never been keen on the idea of the adoption, and aside from a Christmas and birthday package every year, they never contacted Cam about Ellie.

Having Kelly and the girls in Ellie's life gave her some female influences. Cam wished Kelly could spend more time with Ellie, but with her recovering from her husband's death, working full-time, and raising three daughters—a preteen and two teenagers—Kelly simply didn't have it in her to be a consistent mom figure to Ellie as well.

Don't dwell on things you can't change, Reynolds. He arranged the papers on his desk. Allowing Ellie to be feminine stayed at the forefront of his thoughts. She loved princesses and dolls and hair bows and all that other girlie stuff, and Cam feared he'd turn her into a rough-and-tumble tomboy without her mommy around to keep him balanced. He'd enrolled her in ballet classes that would start in a couple of weeks. *Ballet, for goodness' sake.* But he knew she would love it.

The front door of his office creaked open. He glanced at the clock—5:30. He'd forgotten to lock the door. He walked to the front of the shop, looked at the customer, and stopped. He felt his jaw drop. His heart seemed to skip over itself. He couldn't believe who stood in his doorway.

28

Sadie twisted the strap of her purse. The surprised expression on Cam's face relayed his disbelief that she would really take him up on his offer to see Ellie. In truth, she was scared out of her wits at the prospect of seeing the girl. She had no idea what the five-year-old would think of her, the woman who didn't want to be her mommy. But oh, how Sadie wished she could have been Ellie's mother. Day in and day out, she thought of what it would have been like to give the child her baths, to comb her hair, to kiss away boo-boos, to clean up her spilled juice. Sadie knew she couldn't even begin to imagine all the joys and trials she'd missed with her little girl.

And now here she stood, in small-town Delaware, hundreds of miles from the place she'd called home since graduating college. And staring at the man who was raising her daughter. Cam looked just the same as he had five years before. Brown hair, cut short. Short stubbles tracing his chin and jaw but not so long as to cover the deep dimple in his chin. Kind yet inquisitive hazel eyes. Yes, Cam was every bit as handsome as he'd been when Sadie gave birth to Ellie. If anything, he'd grown in girth, the muscles through his shirt appearing larger, stronger than she'd remembered.

She pushed a wayward strand of hair behind her ear. "Hello, Cam."

"Sadie?"

Though he said her name as a question, she knew it was more of a statement, a mixture of shock and disbelief. It was obvious she was the last person on earth he'd expected to see standing in his doorway. Lifting her purse strap up onto her shoulder, Sadie then pressed at the wrinkles in her pencil-straight black skirt. She'd come directly from an interview with the school superintendent. Well, directly was a relative term. In truth, she'd sat in her car in the parking lot for more than an hour trying to muster the courage to drive the route the Internet had given to Cam's place of business.

An inner battle raged over what Cam would think of her arrival in his town. Would he think she was nuts? *Am I nuts? What biological mother tracks down her five-year-old daughter?* She revisited the piercing of her heart, that moment when the nurse took her baby away. There were probably a lot of biological mothers who wanted to track down their children.

Praying every moment, she'd been able to follow the course

and then walk into his office. *What will he think when he learns I accepted a position here in town?* She still couldn't decipher what she thought about it. Never in her wildest imagination would she have thought the superintendent would offer her the occupational therapist position immediately after the interview. It was the middle of May. He had an entire summer to interview candidates, and yet he'd hired Sadie instantly. *And who does that? I've never heard of a superintendent hiring a candidate on the spot. Surely that was from God.*

To her surprise, she'd accepted without a moment's thought. Now that more than an hour had passed, she wondered if she'd accepted too soon. *Maybe I should have prayed more about it. Have I really given this to God? Why did I even think to check that Web site? Lord, it's such a huge decision.* Uncertainty overwhelmed her.

The memory of Lisa's reaction to Sadie's interview slipped into her mind. Her friend had been elated, feeling the opening had to have come from God. At the time, Sadie had joined in her friend's excitement. And for some reason, though she felt anxious about the choice, Sadie also felt content with the decision.

It's kinda like I'm Ruth following Naomi to a land she'd never known. What was it Ruth said? Something like "Where you go, I'll go. Your people will be my people." Well, Lord, I'm not following my mother-in-law. I'm following my daughter. Give me the right words to say.

Sadie cleared her throat. "Thank you for the pictures of Ellie. I was so sorry to hear about Brenda." Unsure what to do with her hands, she allowed her index and middle fingers to trail the long satin ribbon at the waist of her fitted mint green cardigan. The bow came untied, and she quickly retied it.

Cam nodded but didn't reply. He still didn't seem to have registered that she stood in his office. *Maybe I should have called him before I showed up at his office door.*

Sadie swallowed the lump that formed in her throat. "How long has Brenda been gone? I mean. . .what happened? I mean. . ." Sadie stopped. She had no idea what to say to him. *God, help me here!*

"Ten months. Breast cancer."

Cam seemed to have found his tongue, but his shocked expression hadn't changed. Sadie frowned. "I'm sorry, Cam. I didn't know. It must have been so sudden."

"No. She fought for two years."

Two years? Sadie had no idea. Brenda had been sending pictures and long letters, and for two years she'd been battling breast cancer. Why hadn't she told her? Maybe Sadie could have done something to help. At the very least, she could have prayed for Brenda. *Maybe she was afraid I'd show up on her doorstep, as I'm here on Cam's now.*

She pushed back the fear and anxiety that crept into her body. Maybe she shouldn't have taken that job, shouldn't have even looked it up on the Internet in the first place. *God, what am I doing here?*

"What do you want, Sadie?" Cam's voice was monotone, his face without expression.

"To see Ellie." Before Sadie had time to think, the answer slipped from her lips. It was the longing of her heart. To deny it would be like denying her lungs of breath. Who would have imagined an unplanned child whom she'd seen for only a moment would impact her life in such a way? *I did carry her for nine months. I felt her first movements. Was first to hear her heart beating. I can't help but love her.*

Cam leaned against a desk and crossed his arms in front of his chest. He hadn't responded to her answer, and she still couldn't read his expression.

She shifted her weight from one foot to the other. "Your letter mentioned that maybe I could see Ellie. I've been thinking about it and praying about it, and. . .well, I'm not sure how this would work, but I really want to see her."

An unexpected tear slipped down her cheek. She sucked in her breath and wiped it from her cheek. Her heart's greatest yearning lived with this man. It felt as if all her hopes rested in his hands. *God is in control of my life and all that happens in it. Not Cam Reynolds.* The reminder boosted her confidence, and she stood straighter.

"I didn't really expect. . ." Cam stood to his full height, towering over her. His gaze softened, but questions and confusion still lingered behind his eyes. "I don't know if I'm ready. . .or if Ellie would be ready. I need time to think. I'm sure you came a long way, but. . ."

"It's okay. Don't worry about the drive. . ." Once again feeling a bit irrational at the expedient decision to move to Delaware, she stopped herself before mentioning it. She grabbed a pen and paper from her purse and wrote down her number. "This is my cell number. You can call me anytime." She shoved the paper in his hand. Looking up, she stared into his eyes. Once again, she noted the kindness gazing back at her. It quickened her heart and boosted her confidence again. "I know my appearance must come as a shock to you, but I've been praying about this, Cam. Please, promise you will as well."

"I will."

She turned and walked out the door. A sudden peace

squelched the anxiety that dominated her time in his office. God was the Alpha and the Omega, the First and the Last. He was the Beginning and the End. He guided Ruth into an alien land and blessed her with more than she ever would have imagined. He knew what would happen with Sadie and her little girl.

❧

Cam couldn't believe Sadie Ellis had been standing in the doorway of his office only fifteen minutes ago. The teen who had given birth to Ellie no longer looked anything like a teenager. Sadie, with her long dark hair and light green eyes, had grown into a woman. To his chagrin, he'd noticed how long her legs looked in the straight skirt. When she played with the ribbon on her sweater, he couldn't help but take in how trim her waist was. She was ten years his junior. In his mind, Sadie was little more than a girl.

But, wow, how the girl has grown.

He shook his head as he walked up the steps of Kelly's house. The noise he heard inside the walls would keep his mind from such thoughts. He opened the door and was instantly wrapped in a bear hug.

"Hi, Daddy. Aunt Kelly made lasagna. She let me help put garlic on the bread." She scrunched her nose. "Garlic stinks. Like garbage."

She pushed a chunk of hair behind her ear. Something he'd seen her biological mother do only minutes before. Again, he marveled at how much Ellie looked like Sadie. He thought of updating his gun collection before his little girl grew up. If she grew to be as beautiful as Sadie, he'd need to do all he could to keep the boys away.

He pinched her nose. "Garlic stinks, but it tastes good."

Ellie giggled and squirmed away from him. "That's what Aunt Kelly said."

"Ellie!" The voice of one of his nieces yelled from the back of the house. "If you want me to braid your hair, you've got to come here."

"Britty's going to fix my hair." Ellie smiled and raced away. "I'm coming."

Cam chuckled at Ellie's nickname for Kelly's middle daughter. The poor thirteen-year-old's name was Brittany, but since Ellie couldn't pronounce it when she was just a little thing, the whole family took to calling her Britty.

"Hey, Cam." Kelly walked into the living area. "Do you have the gasket for the kitchen sink? The dripping is driving me crazy."

Cam looked at his sister, only two years older than him. She exuded exhaustion and sadness. The sudden death of her husband had taken a toll on her. She and Tim had been married almost eighteen years, since the month after she graduated high school. He'd been with her through the birth of all three of their daughters, as well as supported her through college so that she could get her degree in teaching. When she was only thirty-six, a traffic accident had taken her lifelong sweetheart from her.

"I got it right here." He held up the gasket. "It'll only take a minute to fix." He smiled and sniffed the air. "Something smells awfully good."

A slow smile formed on her lips. "You fix my sink; then I'll feed you."

"Deal."

Cam headed to the sink. Within minutes, the drip was gone, and he and the family enjoyed a dinner of salad, homemade lasagna, and garlic bread. Having practically gorged himself on the home-cooked food, Cam sat back in his chair while Ellie played with Kelly's youngest daughter and the two oldest girls argued over which one would do dishes.

Kelly set a cup of coffee on the table in front of Cam. She settled into the seat beside him.

"Thanks." He took a drink of the strong black coffee. The argument ensued in the kitchen. He cocked one eyebrow. "You going to help those girls decide?"

"Not unless it goes to blows. And if it goes to blows, they're both in a world of trouble."

Cam chuckled at Kelly's response. Six months ago, Tim would have gone in and settled the dispute with no questions asked and no further arguments. The girls seemed to wear Kelly down.

"You want me to handle it?"

Kelly frowned. "No. They're fifteen and thirteen years old. They've always had to help, and now that Tim's gone, I want them to be even more responsible. They have to learn to work together."

Cam nodded and looked back at Ellie and his youngest niece. He couldn't get over how much Ellie looked like Sadie. *What would she think if I allowed her to meet Sadie?* He and Brenda had always been honest with Ellie that she had been adopted. His daughter had always beamed when they told her she had been chosen to be their little girl. A few times, she'd asked about the lady who'd given her birth. The most recent time had been when she'd seen a pregnant woman at the store. But they'd never talked much about Sadie.

"So, Cam, what's up?" Kelly's voice interrupted his thoughts.

He shrugged. "Nothing, I guess."

"Whatever." Kelly swatted the air. "I'm your big sister. I know when something's up."

Cam stared at his sister. As tired and frazzled as she'd become, she was still the caring, intuitive person she'd always been. "Sadie showed up at my office today."

Kelly furrowed her eyebrows. "Sadie? Who's Sadie?" Realization shone on her face. "You don't mean. . . ?" She gazed at Ellie then back at Cam.

Cam nodded. "The one and only. Ellie's birth mother."

"What did she want?"

"To see Ellie."

"Why?"

"I think it's my fault." Cam rubbed his jaw. "Brenda has always sent a letter and pictures to Sadie on Ellie's birthday. Well, of course, this year I sent them." He frowned, trying to remember exactly what he'd written. "I think I told her she could come see Ellie if she wanted. I didn't really mean anything by it. Don't even know why I wrote it. I put the whole envelope together really fast. I haven't had a lot of time lately." He stopped and looked at his sister's face. She twisted the earring in her right ear, a sign that Kelly was thinking.

"What did you tell her?"

"I'd have to think about it."

"Hmm." Kelly continued to twist the earring. "Wasn't Sadie a Christian?"

"Yeah. She seemed like a really good kid. Made a mistake in college. Her parents were less than happy about the situation, and she was kinda stuck on her own. Brenda loved the girl."

"Hmm."

"Mom!" A screech from the kitchen interrupted their conversation. "Brittany is being a jerk." Kelly's oldest daughter,

Zoey, stomped into the dining area. "I did the dishes last night. Just because she vacuumed today doesn't mean I should have to do the dishes again."

Cam watched as irritation wrapped his sister's features. "What chores have you done today, Zoey?"

"Well. . ."

"Well? Nothing. That's what you've done. You've hidden yourself in your room watching movies and talking to your boyfriend on instant messaging. Brittany has picked up the house and played with Ellie. You have the dishes."

The fifteen-year-old redhead stamped her foot. "It's not fair. I did them yesterday."

"It is fair. Now get in the kitchen."

"Mom, you just—"

Kelly pointed her finger at the girl. "Zoey, if you argue with me, I'll take away your instant messaging."

Zoey clamped her lips shut and stomped back into the kitchen. Kelly slumped down into her chair and let out a long breath. "That girl is getting harder and harder to handle."

Cam put his hand on Kelly's. "She's fifteen, and she's just lost her father. It only makes sense that she's getting more difficult to manage."

"You're right, but I'm not sure how much more I can take. Tim was so good with the girls."

Cam squeezed Kelly's hand. "I will help you in any way. You name what I can do."

"You've already done so much, Cam. I'm thankful God gave me a good brother to help me get through this. Did I tell you Mom and Dad are going to take the girls for a few weeks in July?"

Cam smiled. "That will be great, sis. You'll get some time to rest, and they'll love visiting their grandparents in Florida."

"Yeah. That's what Mom said. I think they want Ellie to come, too."

Cam frowned. He didn't know if he was ready to allow Ellie to be away from him for two whole weeks. She'd probably love spending the time with her grandparents and her cousins, but what would he do without her?

Kelly lifted her mug to her lips and took a sip of her coffee. "About Sadie."

Cam's heart sped up. He'd forgotten they'd been talking about her before Zoey threw her fit. He looked at Ellie. Again she pushed a stray hair that had escaped her braids behind her ear, mimicking the gesture Sadie had made. It might be good to allow Ellie to meet Sadie. But what if Sadie decided she didn't want to see Ellie after only one or two visits? He wouldn't allow her to walk in and out of Ellie's life. The child had been through enough with the loss of her mom. And if she really wanted to see Ellie, why wouldn't she have contacted him months or even years before? *I wonder if she ever contacted Brenda.*

He pushed that thought away. Even if her desire to see Ellie was honorable, what had she been doing the last five years? For all Cam knew, she was married with more kids and wanted to steal his little girl out from under him. She could be an alcoholic, be married to a drug dealer, could have spent time in the penitentiary.

"I've been praying about this." Sadie's words slipped through Cam's mind. In his heart, he knew none of those things were true. Call it intuition or maybe the Holy Spirit, but Cam could tell by the way Sadie looked and how she talked that she was being genuine.

"I think you should let them meet." Kelly's words penetrated Cam's mind.

"You do? But what if Sadie doesn't hang around? I don't want Ellie's heart broken."

"Hmm. That's true." Kelly stood and picked up his empty cup. "Maybe you need to pray about it."

Those had been Sadie's words. She'd said she'd been praying about it. He'd told her that he'd pray about it, too. *Maybe I need to do just that.*

three

In only three weeks' time, Sadie had found a cute one-bedroom apartment in small-town Delaware, packed up every belonging she owned, and moved herself hundreds of miles away from all she knew. Her parents hadn't thought much about the move, but they hadn't been overtly involved in Sadie's life. . .well, ever. The singles' group at church had given her a wonderful party that, in some odd way, seemed to confirm her decision to move. Leaving the kids and colleagues from the school system was harder than she'd imagined, and saying good-bye to Lisa's boys had nearly ripped her heart in two. And yet she'd left. Gone. *All for a little girl I'm not at all sure I'll be able to have a relationship with.*

The words of Ruth from the Old Testament flowed through her mind. *"Where you go I will go, and where you stay I will stay. Your people will be my people and your God my God."* Sadie knew she wasn't following her mother-in-law away from a pagan land as Ruth had, and yet she felt very much like a drifter without a goal. Her life's purpose had become the opportunity to have a relationship with the baby she'd held for only brief moments after delivery.

"Where do you want me to put the extra sheets—top shelf or middle shelf?" Lisa's voice sounded from the hall.

"Middle shelf. I'll use the top one for thicker blankets." Having Lisa at the apartment for the last two days had been an enormous help. Not only was her friend a great packer- and unpacker, she also kept Sadie's mind from wandering to thoughts of why Cam hadn't called yet, or what Ellie would think if she saw Sadie, or if Ellie would hate her, or. . .

Organizing dishes in the top oak cabinet, Sadie squelched the fear of rejection that threatened to bring up the sugary, high-calorie breakfast of strong coffee and day-old donuts she'd eaten several hours before. *Now is not the time to worry about what Ellie will think of me. It's time to work. And maybe have a little faith.*

She sliced through the duct tape of another box. As she lifted out a pot and lid, she thought of Cam's expression the night she'd shown up at his office. He seemed more than shocked; something akin to horrified described the way he looked. Shoving the pot into the bottom cabinet, she pushed the remembrance away. She didn't need to worry about Cam's response to seeing her at this moment either. *Have a little faith, Sadie.*

She glanced at her watch. It was nearly lunchtime, and she was determined to finish unpacking the kitchen before she took a break. She noted the two additional large boxes marked KITCHEN that sat mockingly on the linoleum floor beside her. *I might work a little faster if I wasn't thinking about Cam and Ellie every five seconds.*

But she couldn't help it. Three weeks had passed and she still hadn't heard from Cam. She pulled her cell phone from the front pocket of her jean shorts to check for missed calls. *Maybe my phone malfunctioned and didn't ring the call through.*

None. The last call she'd received had been the dental appointment reminder. The one before that had been Rick in a panic because he couldn't find the new package of diapers Lisa had bought before helping Sadie move. *Help me with my faith, Lord.*

She sighed. Who was she kidding? She'd checked her

phone a million or more times since she'd seen Cam. Each time, she told herself she wouldn't check; she'd wait for the ring. Then she'd check again ten minutes later.

If he didn't call by the time she'd completely unpacked— and since he hadn't returned the two, okay, three calls she'd made to him in the last week—then she'd have to pay him another visit. She knew he could deny allowing her to see Ellie. He had every legal right to keep them separated. She knew he probably feared Ellie experiencing more pain on top of Brenda's death. *He may be afraid I'll walk away again.*

The very notion felt like a punch in her stomach. It had nearly killed her giving Ellie away the first time. Now that she was twenty-four and had her degree and a stable job, not to mention a right relationship with the Lord, Sadie could never walk away from Ellie again.

She didn't regret the decision to allow Ellie to be adopted. It had been the right choice at the time, and Sadie's faith in the Lord had grown substantially as a result. *Which is why I must trust Him now.*

The thought nearly brought her to her knees. She placed the casserole dish in her hands on the stove. Gripping the edge of the countertop, she bowed her head. "Oh sweet Jesus, help me to trust in You as I wait for Cam's answer. You put everything in place for me to move here. I know Your hand is in this. I only need to trust You for timing."

❧

"Don't burn me, Daddy," Ellie squealed as she flinched away from the curling iron. The little urchin had found the gadget buried in the back of the bathroom cabinet and had begged him to fix her hair.

Cam blew out a breath as he pulled it away from her. "Ellie, if you flinch like that, it *will* burn you. Hold still."

He gripped her newly cut bangs between his fingers then smashed them with the curling iron. Ellie flinched again, causing him to burn his finger.

"Ouch!" He pulled his hand away, turned on the cold-water faucet, and stuck his finger beneath the cool stream. "Ellie, you have to hold still."

"Sorry, Daddy. You scare me. I can feel the hot on my forehead." She sniffed, and a tear slipped down her cheek.

He felt like an overgrown grump. It wasn't Ellie's fault he had no idea how to work the hair contraption. "It's okay, pun'kin. Why don't we leave the hair fixing to Aunt Kelly and the girls?"

He took in the curls flipping outward at the sides of her bangs. It would be okay—if one side wasn't resting a full inch higher than the other. Poor Ellie looked like someone had taken a hacksaw to her hair. He would never be able to fix them right. *Which is why I didn't want her to get bangs cut in the first place.*

"But my hair looks funny." Ellie puckered her bottom lip and gripped her blanket closer to her chest. "I'll sit still. I promise."

Cam held back the growl that formed in the back of his throat. Brenda would take care of this if she were still alive. Cam was the parent who wrestled with Ellie in the yard, taught her how to catch a ball, and drenched her with the water hose as they cleaned the truck. He didn't know any daddies who curled their daughters' hair.

But then, he didn't know any daddies raising their little girls alone. *Ah, Brenda, this is only one of the many ways I miss you.*

In the two years she'd battled cancer, several times he'd prayed, sought God, and even come to terms with the knowledge that he would miss Brenda's touch as a woman.

He knew he'd miss her help as caretaker of their home and Ellie. But he hadn't been prepared for how hard it would be to teach Ellie about the feminine side of life. Let's face it, what did he know about being a girl?

Sure, Kelly was a part of Ellie's life. And through the summer, Kelly and the girls planned to spend a good amount of time with Ellie. But fall would come. And when it did, Kelly would be swamped with her girls and teaching. Cam had no choice but to do the "girly" things with Ellie.

With a snarl, he picked up the curling iron then grabbed a piece of her hair and quickly pulled it through the iron. Fifteen minutes later, her hairstyle wasn't great, but it was presentable. That was all he could give her.

"All done, Daddy." Ellie raced out of the bathroom. He heard the television turn on, and the theme song of one of her favorite cartoons pealed through the air.

Cam placed his finger under a stream of cold water once more. A large water blister had already formed, stinging more than he would have thought. *Who would have known fixing hair could be so dangerous?* He swallowed back an ironic chuckle that formed. He'd smashed every one of his fingers, torn off nails, and attained more cuts, scrapes, and bruises than he could count at his job; but a little bitty curling iron burn had him putting his finger under a stream of water. *Talk about stealing a man's testosterone. I need some manly activities in my life.*

He grunted like Tim Allen from one of his favorite old sitcoms, *Home Improvement*. Before the grunt ended, he heard the ranting and raving of his sister and her daughters as they bounded through the front door. He rubbed his temples with his fingertips. *Nothing like a house full of women to make a guy feel like a man.*

❧

Sadie checked the miles she'd driven against the miles left to Cam's house. According to the directions she'd printed off the Internet, she didn't have far to go. She and Lisa had finished unpacking her things the day before. They'd enjoyed a wonderful girl night of pizza, popcorn, and movies. Early this morning, Lisa left to head back to North Carolina. Afterward, Sadie spent the rest of the morning in prayer. Cam still hadn't called, but she could wait no longer. She had to do something. She didn't have to talk to Ellie, but maybe if she just drove by their house, just saw where Ellie lived. *He's going to think I'm a stalker.* She placed a hand on her chest. *I would think I was a stalker, but waiting on him is killing me.*

Peering out the windshield, she noted the serenity of nature around her. The land looked like grass-covered ocean waves, rolling high and low on each side. Large, lush trees covered much of the ground without cluttering it. Occasionally, she passed a large pond. Delaware was every bit as beautiful as the Smoky Mountains in North Carolina, just in a different way—a way she could easily get used to.

Just ahead, Sadie spotted a stone house with a room built onto the side. The exterior walls of the room were made of nothing but windows. At first glance, she thought the room was a patio; but as she drove closer, she noted the lattices in the windows. *Maybe it's a library.*

She recalled the home of one of her high school friends that had an elaborate library. Two walls were covered with bookshelves. The other two walls were windows opening the room to a glorious, mountainous view. The room had seemed to be the most amazing escape, and Sadie had thought she'd want a room just like it in her own home one day. *I haven't thought about Rachael in years. I wonder how she's doing.*

Sadie glanced at her mileage again. She was getting closer. Thoughts of high school girlfriends slipped from her mind. One of the next few houses should be Cam and Ellie's. Her heart began to beat faster beneath her chest. She took deep breaths in and out. What would Ellie think of her? If she was discovered, what would Cam think about her driving by his house? Would he think she had been watching them for days?

A man stood in the front yard of the first house on this street, holding a large shovel in his hands. He wore a T-shirt that he seemed to have outgrown many years before, a pair of dirt-covered denim shorts, and sandals. The muscles in his arms glistened in the sun. Sadie couldn't help but admire the strength those muscles implied. The man scooped mulch from the back of a truck and walked toward one of the many flower beds dispersed across the meticulously landscaped yard.

She drove closer and peered out the passenger window as she passed the house. The man turned his face slightly to the right. It was Cam.

Sadie swallowed the lump that had formed in her throat. *Cam Reynolds is hot!* She shook the thought away. She had not driven all the way out here, had not moved all the way from North Carolina, because Cam Reynolds was a good-looking man. Building a relationship with Ellie was her goal.

After pulling into the next house's driveway, she turned around and headed back toward Cam. Thankfully, several acres separated the houses, and Sadie had a few moments to settle her racing heart before she pulled into his driveway. *So much for just driving by.* She inwardly berated herself. *But it's his fault. He told me I could see Ellie in his letter; then he won't call me back!*

A cold sweat broke out over her body as she inched toward

his house. Dizziness enveloped her, and she released long, slow breaths through her lips. She opened her water bottle and took a quick drink. *Calm down, Sadie. You can do this.*

Fear wrapped itself around her and tunneled throughout her body. She could only imagine what Ellie would think of her. What if she said she hated Sadie? And Cam. He hadn't called her. For all she knew, he would call the police, put out a restraining order, or do whatever he needed to do to keep her from Ellie.

What if Ellie hadn't been told she was adopted?

Sadie hadn't thought of that. Brenda had always told Sadie that she and Cam were honest with Ellie about her being adopted, but then again, Brenda hadn't told Sadie that she had cancer. Maybe Brenda lied about having told Ellie. If Sadie showed up on Cam's doorstep, she may crush all that her little girl had ever known to be true in her life.

Unexpected tears traced down her cheeks. *God, what do I do? I didn't think this through all the way. I should have waited for Cam's call. Oh God, I'm so sorry.*

Sadie brushed the tears away with her fingertips as she drove closer to Cam's house. Determined to head back to her apartment and wait for his call, she snuck one last peek at his house. She drove at little more than a crawl, but she couldn't stop herself. Maybe she would see a glimpse of Ellie. The child would just think a lady passed by in her car.

Cam turned around. Their gazes locked for a brief moment; then he motioned for her to come over. Swallowing the knot in her throat, she tapped the top of the steering wheel, begging God to guide her through this encounter with Cam and her daughter. Sucking in a deep breath, Sadie stepped out of the car.

"Hello, Cam." Her gaze strayed from his face to his sun-kissed biceps. His muscles bragged their hard work. Pushing a strand of hair behind her ear, she forced her gaze away.

A slight sigh escaped Cam's mouth, and she looked back into his eyes. She was always taken aback at the kindness behind his eyes. He threw the shovel into the back of his truck. "I think I need a break. Why don't you come on in, Sadie?"

"Is. . .is Ellie here?"

"No, she's not."

Sadness mixed with relief as Sadie followed Cam into his house. She took in the historic furnishings of the home, displayed in several hues of browns and greens. The house had a manly feel to it, but touches of lace and satin in the curtains and pillows tattled of a woman's touch. "Your home has such a peaceful feel to it."

The words slipped from her lips before she'd had a chance to think them through. He looked around the room as if he was seeing it for the first time in a long time. He gazed back at Sadie. "Thanks."

She followed him into the kitchen. He grabbed a towel out of the laundry basket that sat on the floor beside a door and wiped off the sweat from his forehead. He motioned for her to have a seat at a small table, and she obliged. Wordlessly, she watched as he washed his hands and then opened the refrigerator and pulled out a can of soda. "You want a drink?"

Thinking to decline, she licked her parched lips and thought better of it. "Sure."

He pulled out another drink and set it on the table in front of her. With complete ease, he slid into the chair across from her. He popped open his can and took a long swig. "I guess we need to talk."

Sadie nodded. She struggled to open her soda. Her nerves

had gotten the better of her the last few weeks, and she'd bitten her fingernails well past the tips of her fingers. In one motion, Cam swiped her drink and popped the top. He handed it to her, and she took a slow sip.

He rubbed his stubble-clad jaw. "Where to start?"

"Does Ellie know she's adopted?" The question came out fast, and Sadie watched as Cam frowned.

"Yes. Why?"

Relief washed over Sadie. "I just. . . I. . ." She wrapped her fingers around the can, allowing its cold wetness to calm her nerves. "I so wanted to see her. Then when I passed your house, I had this sinking feeling. . .that maybe she didn't even know."

"Brenda told you from the beginning that we would tell her."

"Yes, but I didn't know about her cancer, and I just thought. . . I mean, I was afraid. . ."

"That she lied." Pain etched his face.

"I didn't mean it like that. I can only imagine how hard it would be to tell your child that you were unable to have one. I mean, on your own."

An expression wrapped his face that Sadie couldn't decipher. He scooped up his soda, taking a long gulp. "You have no idea. But that's not what we need to talk about."

"No." Sadie folded her hands on the table, willing herself to have courage. "Cam, I want the opportunity to have a relationship with Ellie."

He didn't respond, simply studied her for several moments. Finally, he nodded. "I know. But why?"

Why? Why! I've spent the last five years of my life mourning that child. That's why! "Cam, I love Ellie. I have loved her from the moment I knew I carried her in my womb. At nineteen, without support from my boyfriend and with minimal support from my parents, I couldn't keep her." She looked into Cam's eyes, begging him to believe she was telling the truth. "I know God provided you and Brenda for Ellie. You were such a great guy, and Brenda was such an amazing. . .God-fearing woman."

She looked down at the soft drink on the table and chased the condensation down the can with her fingertips. Her heart broke with the knowledge of Brenda's death. She couldn't imagine how Cam and Ellie felt. She gazed back into Cam's eyes. She could see how much he missed Brenda reflected in those hazel pools.

"I'm twenty-four now, Cam. I've spent the last five years of my life finishing school and then working with children in a school system in North Carolina. I've helped my dear friend with her twin boys the last two years. I cooked and cleaned while her husband worked double shifts and she was on bed rest. And I. . ." Sadie took a deep breath. Her nerves were getting the best of her. "Now I have a job here in Delaware. . . ."

"You have a job in Delaware?"

She smiled. "In this very county. I've already moved into a new apartment. I live here."

His eyes widened at her words, and she couldn't hold back a slight nervous giggle. "I've left everything I've known to be closer to Ellie. I kinda feel like Ruth following Naomi to her homeland." She swiped her hand through the air. "Never mind the Ruth stuff. I just can't help but hope that God has given me an opportunity to get to know my little girl."

Silence weighed the room down thicker than a foggy morning in the Smokies. Sadie took a sip of the soda and forced it down her throat.

Cam traced the top of his can with his fingertip. The gesture made the can's top seem surprisingly small beneath his fingers. "What happens when you get married?"

Sadie blinked several times. Married? She didn't have a boyfriend, didn't even want one. Not yet anyway. The few guys she'd dated since Ellie's father had been wonderful, God-fearing men, but they just didn't seem to be right for Sadie. In truth, she'd kept herself so busy with work, odds-and-ends ministries at church, and helping Lisa that she hadn't thought much about it. Sure, she'd gone on practically every singles' outing at church, but the guys there had been more like buddies than anything. "Why would. . . That wouldn't change how I feel about Ellie."

Cam sat back in his chair. "What about when your husband's job has to move him somewhere else? What about when you have other kids?"

Sadie frowned. She hadn't really thought about what would happen if she got married and had children. It was true that one day she did want to marry. She did want children. It would be quite unusual to be Mom to children who lived with her and her husband and be Mom to Ellie who lived with Cam. "Honestly, Cam, I hadn't thought about that." She searched her mind and heart for what she was feeling. "But I can't imagine loving Ellie any less."

Without thinking, she touched her stomach. "She'd still be my firstborn child. Her kicks were the first ones I'd ever felt. Her cries were the first I'd ever heard. That will never change."

Cam stared at her. He didn't move a muscle, didn't even flinch. Sadie's heart sank as she feared he'd already decided not to allow her to be part of Ellie's life.

"I am in control of the universe. Have faith in Me."

The Spirit's reminder lifted her heart. She could trust her heavenly Father. She would trust Him. Cam had all legal rights to Ellie, but God's will was in control of all the earth.

He loved Ellie even more than Sadie did. If it was God's will for Sadie to have a relationship with her little girl, He would make it happen. "I trust you, Lord."

"What was that?"

Sadie gasped. She hadn't realized she'd said her prayer aloud. She shook her head. "Nothing. Just a little prayer."

Cam leaned forward, resting his elbows on the table. "Okay. Here's the deal. Let's start off slow."

Sadie's heart leaped within her, and she couldn't stop the quick, quiet clap of her hands. "Okay."

Cam's mouth bowed into a slow, hesitant grin. "How about you come to our church on Sunday? We'll take you to lunch afterward."

"That sounds great." Sadie stood and lifted her purse strap to her shoulder. "What church do you go to?"

"First Community." Cam stood and guided Sadie to the door. "But, Sadie, let's not tell Ellie who you are. Not just yet."

Sadie's heart plummeted. She wanted to wrap her arms around the little girl, smother her with kisses, and assure her that her biological mother had loved and prayed for her every day of her life. But Sadie allowed his words to sink into her spirit. She nodded. Maybe taking things slowly would be for the best.

four

Cam brushed a piece of lint off his khaki pants. Sadie still hadn't arrived, and church would begin in less than fifteen minutes. He looked beside him at Ellie. She sat in the pew with one leg crossed beneath her and her attention focused on the coloring sheet in her lap, a picture of Jesus surrounded by a group of children. Her bangs looked a little crooked again this morning. The left side had a mind of its own. No matter how many times he smashed it with the curling iron, it always bounced up higher than the right on Ellie's forehead.

He glanced at his watch again. He'd chosen a pew farther back from where he and Ellie normally sat. Assuming Sadie would already be nervous about seeing Ellie, he didn't want to add to her anxiety by having to greet the entire congregation as she made her way to the front of the church. *If she doesn't hurry up, I'll have to introduce her to Ellie after the service.*

Thoughts of what the congregation would think of Sadie had already plagued him through the night. Ellie looked so much like her biological mother that people were bound to make assumptions. The church already knew Ellie had been adopted. He shifted in his seat. Long ago, he'd learned that a man shouldn't worry about things he had no control over, and what the congregation thought of Sadie was out of his hands.

At least Kelly and the girls are at home. It wasn't that he wanted his nieces to be sick; he just didn't want them to meet Sadie. Not yet anyway.

Stealing another peek at the door, he sucked in his breath.

Sadie stood in the entrance. She greeted one of the deacons and took the offered bulletin from his hand. Her dark hair flowed long and silky past her right shoulder. She wore a frilly white blouse that accentuated her trim figure. Her green and white skirt flowed out from the middle of her knees. She looked like she'd just finished modeling for a catalog, and once again, Cam noted how much she'd grown up since Ellie's birth. He tore his gaze away from her. *What are you thinking, Reynolds? The girl is ten years younger than you.*

Clearing his throat and his head, he looked back at her. She saw him and smiled. Her gaze immediately fell beside him. He noted her gasp when she saw Ellie. Fear draped across her features, and she looked back up at him. Cam tried to calm her with a smile. He motioned her toward them. When she reached the pew, he took her hand in his. Ignoring how soft her skin felt, he greeted her. "Hello, Sadie. It's good to see you this morning."

"Hello, Cam." Her voice sounded weak, and her hand shook slightly.

"Ellie?" His daughter looked up from her coloring, and Cam heard Sadie's slight gasp. "I'd like you to meet a. . .friend of mine. This is Sadie Ellis."

Ellie grinned. "Hi. Your name sounds like mine." She placed her hand over her mouth as she giggled.

Sadie leaned over. "Yes, it does." She touched Ellie's hand. "I'm new to this church. Can I sit with you?"

Ellie pushed her crayons and papers farther down the pew. "Yeah. But I go to children's church in minute." She looked up at Cam. "Daddy, can Ms. Ellie sit with you?"

Cam could feel Sadie relax as she grinned at Ellie. "My last name is Ellis, not Ellie. But why don't you call me Sadie."

"Okay, Sadie." Ellie scooted down the pew. "Can Sadie sit with us?"

Cam looked at Sadie. Delight topped the contentment that framed her expression. In an instant, he knew the choice had been right to allow Sadie the opportunity to see Ellie. "Of course she can sit with us."

Sadie settled in beside Ellie. She oohed and aahed over the coloring Ellie had already done. Sadie picked up one of the crayons and began to color with his daughter. Cam glanced around the packed sanctuary. With the church bursting at the seams and the pastor's extended family from New York visiting, no one seemed to notice the new woman sitting beside him. The music began and Ellie popped up from her seat. She grabbed Sadie's hand and helped her stand. Complete bliss filled the woman's expression.

After several songs of praise music, the children were dismissed to their church. Cam watched as Ellie hugged Sadie good-bye then flitted past him and down the aisle toward her teacher.

Sadie's soft hand wrapped around his own. Surprised, he turned toward her. Her face was mere inches from his. She mouthed the words "Thank you." Tears glistened in her light green eyes, displaying her happiness and vulnerability. A primal instinct within him that he thought had died with Brenda forged its way to the front. He wanted to grab her in his arms and kiss the tears away, to share her joy and soothe her fears.

Blinking the thought away, he nodded. She released his hand, and he felt overwhelmingly weak from the loss of her touch. With full effort, he focused on his preacher's moving lips. If only he could actually hear what the man said. The only noise he could decipher was the pulsing beat of his heart pounding in his eardrums.

❧

Sadie could hardly comprehend that she sat at a table directly across from her daughter. Church had ended half an hour before and Cam had taken them to one of Ellie's favorite restaurants. He'd promised Ellie she could play in the play area once she'd finished her lunch. While Cam got them some napkins and ketchup, Sadie studied the child.

Ellie took a big bite of her hamburger then washed it down with a large gulp of her soda. Sadie noted the hint of fatigue through the determination on Ellie's face. Without a doubt, the child would eat, play awhile, and then take a good long nap when she got home.

Oh, how Sadie wished she could cuddle up next to Ellie for a Sunday afternoon nap.

Ellie's resemblance to Sadie was uncanny. Her long dark hair with hints of waves and curls, her slightly upturned nose, even the shape of her eyes—nearly everything about Ellie looked like Sadie. The only difference was that Ellie's eyes were a rich brown, a shade lighter than Sadie's ex-boyfriend's had been, and Sadie's eyes were light green.

Ellie wore a yellow sundress with a large sunflower on the chest. Sadie loved the color on her. She remembered seeing the dress in one of the department stores in North Carolina. As Ellie grew, Sadie couldn't help but browse the children's department of the stores. Many times, she'd picked out clothes, believing Ellie would be such-and-such size. She would hold them as she walked through the store, enjoying the texture of the materials, considering which would be most comfortable to wear. Finally, when it was time for her to leave, she would put them back where they belonged on the rack. She longed to buy cute outfits for Ellie. The little sundress was one Sadie would have picked out. "I like your dress, Ellie."

Ellie wiped her mouth with the back of her hand. Sadie grabbed a napkin as Cam sat beside his daughter. "Don't wipe with your arm, Ellie," he reprimanded. "Use a napkin."

Ellie nodded and swallowed her bite of food. "Aunt Kelly got this for me." She hopped down and twirled in a circle. "It's a twirly dress."

"Yes, it's very pretty." Cam lifted her back on her chair. "But we don't need to twirl right now. We need to eat."

Sadie couldn't help but grin at Ellie's exaggerated pout. "Your daddy's right. You need to eat. But your dress is definitely pretty."

She shifted in her chair again. "Aunt Kelly got me another dress. It's red and has a ladybug on it."

"I bet it's pretty, too. Does your Aunt Kelly live around here?"

Cam wiped ketchup from Ellie's mouth. He crumpled the napkin and laid it on the table. "Yeah. Kelly's my sister. She and her three girls just moved here a few months ago."

"Uncle Tim went to see Mommy in heaven." Ellie took another drink then jumped off the chair. "Can I play now, Daddy?"

"Sure. Take off your shoes and put them in one of the slots. Sadie and I will be right here."

Sadie frowned at what Ellie had said. Had Cam's sister's husband passed away as well? Before she could think more about it, Ellie had slipped off her shoes and bounded inside the massive jungle gym.

"My sister's husband died this year." Cam's voice was low, just over a whisper.

"I'm sorry."

"It was a car accident." He leaned back in the chair. Sadie followed his gaze to the ball pit. Ellie waved at them, and they waved back. "It's been a hard year. A lot of loss."

Sadie didn't know what to say. She'd never really had to deal with death. Even though their relationship had been strained the last five years, both of her parents were still alive. She didn't have any siblings, and she'd grown up away from her grandparents. When her mother's dad and her father's parents passed away, she'd felt only some sadness. "I'm so sorry for all of you."

Cam looked at her. "Ellie misses Brenda, but she's dealt with her death better than I ever would have anticipated. Now she's watching her aunt and cousins grieve their husband and daddy. She doesn't need any more loss."

Sadie swallowed. A part of her felt offended that he would insinuate or, worse, believe that she would walk into Ellie's life and then turn around and walk back out. Sadie had every intention of being a mother to Ellie. She knew it sounded crazy, even in her own mind. How could a woman give up her baby and then five years later decide she wanted her back?

But Sadie did want her back.

She didn't want to take Ellie from Cam. Cam was Ellie's father, in nearly every sense of the word. He cared for Ellie, nurtured Ellie, loved her. It was obvious he'd been a terrific dad, and Sadie felt blessed that God had provided Cam and Brenda for Ellie.

But the situation had changed.

Sadie never would have taken Brenda from Ellie. If she had known, Sadie would have prayed tirelessly for Brenda's healing. Sadie cared for Brenda. She considered her somewhat of a friend, a sister in Christ. Sadie knew Brenda loved Ellie as if she'd been her biological mother.

But death had physically separated Ellie and Brenda. With

a confidence of spirit that overwhelmed Sadie at times, she knew God wanted her to be in Delaware, near her little girl. "Cam, I promise you I will do nothing to hurt Ellie."

He nodded, but she noted the uncertainty that still lurked in his eyes. Sadie wished she could say something to put his mind at ease, but she knew he would need time to see that she wasn't going anywhere.

"Daddy, I. . ."

Sadie's heart dropped as Ellie limped toward their table, tears welling in her eyes. In a flash, Sadie hopped out of her chair and lifted Ellie into her arms. She pushed the wrappings away from the table, giving her a place to set Ellie down and check the damage to her leg. Sadie gingerly touched her foot and examined both sides of her ankle. "Let's see, sweetie. I don't see any. . ."

A slight chuckle sounded from Cam, and Sadie looked up to see Cam covering his mouth with his hand as Ellie's eyes widened. The child sniffed and gawked at Sadie. "I hurt my toe."

Sudden heat raced up Sadie's neck as she took in the barely visible scratch. The skin hadn't even broken. Knowing she'd overreacted, she clicked her tongue. "You're fine. Just a scratch."

Cam picked her up. "I'd say she's more tired than hurt."

"I'm not tired," Ellie whined, obviously deciding to go with the notion that she'd been maimed in some way. "I'm hurt."

"Okay." Cam smoothed her hair with his free hand. "Let's see if the hurt goes away after we take a nap."

"I don't want a nap."

Sadie cleaned up the wrappings off the table and threw them in the trash. She followed Cam and Ellie out the door and stopped at his truck. She'd driven herself, so this was apparently the end of the visit. She ran her fingers through the bottom of Ellie's hair. "I was glad to meet you, Ellie."

Ellie turned to face Sadie, her eyes puffy from crying. "I don't want a nap."

Sadie touched her cheek. "You know what, I'm probably going to take a nap, too."

Ellie looked at Cam. "Daddy, can Sadie take a nap with us?"

Ellie's innocent statement planted a picture in Sadie's mind, and she quickly shook it away. Looking at Cam, she thought he'd imagined the same thing. "I don't think so, pun'kin." His voice sounded scratchy, and he cleared his throat.

"I'd love to see you another time." Sadie tried to convey the urgency she felt to see Ellie again through her gaze.

Ellie perked up, grabbing Cam's jaw with her hands. "Can she go fishing with us, Daddy?"

Sadie grimaced, and Cam laughed. "I think that's a great idea, pun'kin." He cocked one eyebrow. "Will you go fishing with us this Thursday evening?"

Fishing was definitely not her forte. But Sadie would do anything to be close to Ellie. "Sure. Just tell me when and where."

"My house. Seven thirty."

"You got it." She patted Ellie's back. "I'll see you then." Sadie slipped into her car. Seeing Ellie had been bliss. She could hardly wait for Thursday to come. *As long as I don't have to touch a worm or a fish, I will be perfectly content.* She bit the inside of her lip. If that was what she had to do to see Ellie, she wouldn't complain.

five

Cam dropped the handsaw to the ground then scratched the beard that had formed over the past four days. *I've got to get Sadie out of my mind.* He measured the wood with his tape measure. "I cut half an inch more than I should have."

He threw the tape measure into his toolbox. "It's all this daydreaming." He growled as he leaned back against the wall of his garage. *A man shouldn't spend his time thinking about silky brown hair; long legs; a trim waist; and eyes, so full of determination, gazing at him through green orbs.*

He pushed away from the wall. "What has gotten into you, Reynolds?"

"What *has* gotten into you, Cam?" Kelly's voice sounded from the front of the garage. She walked to his worktable. "Weren't you working on this two days ago?"

He folded his arms in front of his chest. "Yep."

"Did you say you cut this piece too short?"

"I did."

"As I recall, the last time my brother messed up his woodworking was when he was falling for a cute little blond by the name of Brenda."

Cam grunted. "What is that supposed to mean?"

"It means even when Brenda was sick, even after she died, you stayed focused on your work. If anything, your pieces turned out to be near perfection." Kelly sat on the stool. "So what's going on? Does it have to do with Sadie?"

"I don't know." Cam shrugged. "Just because the woman

wants to step in and be a mother figure in Ellie's life?" His voice dripped with sarcasm as he waved his hands in front of his chest and shook his head. "No. That's not stressing me out in the slightest."

Kelly peered at him for several moments. He wondered if the temperature in the room rose several degrees. Kelly furrowed her eyebrows. "I don't think that's all of it."

"Whatever." Cam picked up another piece of wood. He measured the appropriate length and penciled a mark. He knew he was being abrupt with Kelly, but he wasn't ready to admit to himself the feelings he was experiencing, let alone talk about them with his sister.

"Ellie said she met a pretty lady named Sadie at church on Sunday." Kelly's voice took on a winsome tone. "She said Sadie liked her dress and that she colored a picture with her and that she was coming to the house to fish tonight."

Cam measured the wood again to double-check his mark was right. "Yeah, so?"

"I'm assuming Ellie doesn't know who Sadie is."

Cam peeked back at Kelly then picked up the handsaw. "No, she doesn't. I want them to see each other a few times first."

"Zoey thinks Sadie must be your girlfriend for you to be introducing her to Ellie."

"Humph." Panic welled within Cam. Zoey would be surprised to know just how much a part of Cam wished that to be true. Logically, it made no sense. And Cam had to keep telling himself to think logically. He scratched the top of his head then rubbed his jaw.

"Just as I feared."

He turned and looked at Kelly. "What are you talking about?"

"You scratched your head and then rubbed your jaw."

"So?"

"So. You always do that when you're trying to hide something."

"Trying to what?"

Kelly stood and walked to Cam. She rested her hand on his arm. "You're attracted to Sadie, aren't you?"

It was on the tip of his tongue to lie, but his spirit stopped him. He slumped back against the wall. "I guess I am."

Kelly nodded and walked out the garage door. "I'll be praying for you, little brother. Have fun tonight."

He stood back to his full height, rested the blade against the wood, and then second-guessed himself. Picking up the tape measure, he knew he would have to check the length one more time to ensure he'd marked correctly. All this girlie daydreaming was interfering with his and Ellie's livelihood.

Pray for me about tonight. She'd better be praying. Between his raging emotions and Sadie's amazing looks and adorable excitement with Ellie, he had no doubt he would need all the prayers he could get.

❧

Sadie stared at Cam and Ellie's house. Her nerves were getting the best of her. Flattening the wrinkles from her new khaki shorts, she remembered the red hat she'd purchased to go with the ladybug sundress that Ellie's aunt had bought her.

One of the advantages of her new state was no sales tax, and Sadie had made full use of the perk over the last few days. Owning only dressy casual clothes, she'd had no idea what to wear on a fishing trip, and she was sure her grunge/bedtime clothes covered with stains and holes would not be appropriate. Venturing into the largest city in Delaware, Sadie had made her way to the Concord Mall. In North Carolina, she'd had to drive over an hour to get to a shopping mall, so she intended to relish the ninety or so stores in the mall. With plans to buy something casual and cheap to wear, she found herself strolling through some of the children's stores selecting cute outfits for Ellie. With no sales tax, she would have been able to purchase more than she'd intended.

Of course, after she'd picked up a dress and two short outfits, Sadie had come to her senses and put them back. Ellie wouldn't know what to think of a nearly perfect stranger buying her a bunch of clothes. *I'm not sure Cam would have appreciated it either.*

Unable to keep herself from buying something for her daughter, Sadie selected an adorable fisherman's style hat to match Ellie's dress. Then she'd made her way to the women's department to find her khaki shorts and T-shirt.

Exhaling a deep breath, Sadie scooped the hat out of the passenger's seat of her car and headed for the front door. She'd barely reached the step when Ellie bounded out onto the porch.

"Hey, Sadie."

The child's hair was fixed in two flat braids that rested over the front of her shoulders. She wore the sweetest red and white gingham shirt and little blue jean shorts. Sadie wanted to lift her little girl into her arms and squeeze her with the pent-up love she'd held back for so long. *Patience, Sadie. She has no idea who you are, and if she found out right now, it would probably scare her to death.*

Sadie leaned over and flipped a braid around Ellie's shoulder. "Hey, Ellie. You look like you're ready to go fishing."

Ellie nodded then grabbed Sadie's hand. She practically dragged Sadie into the house. "Daddy, Sadie's here. We can go now."

Cam walked out of the kitchen wiping his hands on a dishrag. "Perfect timing. I just finished cleaning up the kitchen."

Sadie held back a whistle. There was something over-the-top enticing about a man big as a Smoky Mountain bear with a full-grown beard and a masculine glint in his eye who was holding a dishrag having just finished the kitchen work. Cam Reynolds would be a better catch than any finned creature they might see at his pond.

What is wrong with me? Sadie shook the wayward thought from her mind. *I can't think about Cam that way. He's the father of my daughter.* She pursed her lips. *Okay, that didn't sound right. But he is ten years older than I am.*

She snuck another peek at him. He had squatted down in front of Ellie to tie her shoelaces. *What is ten years when a man looks like that?*

"Stop it," she muttered.

"What's that?" Cam looked up at her.

Heat flooded Sadie's cheeks and neck. She looked down at the hat in her hand. "Oh, Ellie. I almost forgot. I bought this for you."

Ellie skipped back over to Sadie. She took the hat from Sadie's hands, placed it on her head, and then looked at Cam. "Look, Daddy. Aren't I pretty?"

"You sure are."

"Am I as pretty as Sadie?"

Sadie sucked in her breath. What had beguiled the child to say that? She glanced at Cam, noting his beard didn't mask the red that spilled across his cheeks. "I would say you are."

Sadie cleared her throat. "Ellie, I got that hat to go with the red dress your aunt bought you."

"My ladybug dress?"

Sadie nodded. She snuck a peek at Cam, whose posture visibly relaxed with the change of subject. "Did you know the ladybug is your state bug?"

Ellie scrunched her nose. "Our state bug? What's a state bug?"

"It's the bug that represents Delaware."

"What's 'represents' mean, Daddy?"

Cam chuckled. "It kinda means it shows who we are."

Ellie shoved one of her braids into her mouth. Sadie thought to tell her not to eat her hair, but decided if Cam didn't mind, she shouldn't correct her child either. *Her* child—Sadie couldn't stop thinking of Ellie as her child. Biologically, she was. Now all Sadie could think about was living out being a mother to Ellie as well.

Ellie pulled her hair from her mouth. A frown still etched her face. "You mean I am a ladybug?"

Cam laughed out loud.

"But I don't want to be a bug, Daddy." Ellie reached up and grabbed Cam's hand. "I don't like bugs."

Sadie didn't know what to say. She regretted even mentioning the state bug thing. How did one explain a state bug to a child? *Ellie's right. Why in the world does a state need a bug as a mascot?*

"No, sweetie." Sadie searched her mind for an explanation a five-year-old would understand. "It's not that you're a bug. Each state has a bug, a flower, a flag—all kinds of things that represent who they are. For Delaware, the state bug just happens to be a ladybug. Probably, there are a lot of ladybugs living in Delaware. . . ."

Cam lifted Ellie over his right shoulder then turned to Sadie and smiled. The man could make her lose all sense of reality when he looked at her like that. "Don't worry, Sadie.

Ellie here *is* a ladybug."

He held her with his right hand and tickled her belly with his left. Ellie folded over into uncontrollable giggles.

Sadie brushed a piece of hair away from her face. "Thanks for saving me."

"You're welcome." Cam put Ellie down and picked up a container that she assumed to be his tackle box. "So where'd you learn that ladybugs are our state bug?"

Sadie rolled her eyes. "My landlord. He knows everything about the state of Delaware and wants to be sure I know how fortunate I am to live here."

Cam's gaze softened. "No, *we're* fortunate you live here."

Sadie's heart felt as if it had melted beneath her lungs. He was glad to have her around. He was giving her the opportunity to get to know her daughter. *Sweet Jesus, You are too good to me. Thank You for softening his heart.*

❧

With a bottle of lemon-flavored water in his hand, Cam settled onto the metal bench that he'd placed some fifteen feet from the pond. The cool June air rested on him with more comfort than a long, soothing sit in a hot tub after a day of hard manual labor. The sun had set a little more than an hour before, and Ellie had been sound asleep for about as long. Again, he was thankful the pond was so near the back of the house. He couldn't count the times he'd sat in this very spot, sometimes for several hours, after Ellie had gone to sleep. Sometimes he'd mourned Brenda's death. Other times he'd praised God for a blessing of some kind. This spot was the place he did most of his talking, and listening, to God.

The water lay still and peaceful with only an occasional fish popping up his head to snatch at a bug of some kind that had landed on the water. He grinned at the memory of the evening he and Ellie had spent with Sadie.

"Are we catching weakfish today? I've heard they're the Delaware state fish," Sadie had asked while she held the fishing rod he'd given her at an odd angle. He'd feared she would hook herself or one of them before the trip ended.

"Weakfish are saltwater fish," he'd responded.

"Oh." She'd lifted her eyebrows then furrowed them deep into a frown. She'd had no idea what he was talking about. Her confused expression made her even more attractive.

"A pond has freshwater in it."

She'd pushed her head back, her lips forming the cutest O he'd ever seen. "I see."

Cam laughed out loud. She didn't "see." It was apparent she didn't have a clue what he meant.

"Daddy, are we fish now, too?" Ellie'd grown as confused as Sadie.

Leaning back on the bench, Cam smiled at the memory. He took a drink of water then wiped his mouth with the back of his hand. He'd had more fun today than he'd had in years.

It pained him to think that way. He'd loved Brenda, had poured his heart, body, soul, and mind into their relationship. God commanded him to love Brenda as Christ loved the church, with a willingness to give his life for her. He'd heeded God's command, not only out of obedience, but also out of a true, deep desire. She had been all he'd ever wanted in a spouse.

Still, he couldn't deny the last two years of her life had been hard ones. The surgery, the chemo, the radiation had taken a toll on her physically and emotionally. Brenda had been a real trooper the entire time, and her good days were really good. But the bad days had been misery to endure.

Guilt stabbed him at the joy he'd felt fishing today. Sadie was very different from Brenda, in looks, in personality, but Cam found himself drawn to the younger woman.

He leaned forward, resting his elbows on his knees. It felt wrong to think of Sadie that way. He felt unfaithful to Brenda. In only a few weeks, it would be one year since her death. He'd never imagined he would find himself so drawn to another woman. Not only did he feel guilt, but part of him also felt selfish. He knew plenty of people who never found the right person to cherish for all their lives, and here he was contemplating a second.

He huffed. *What am I thinking? Contemplating a second? I barely know Sadie. My feelings are probably simply a man's natural reaction to a beautiful, sweet lady after his wife's been gone awhile. I'm not some young pup who can't think with his mind.*

He stood, stretching the kinks out of his arms and back. *Maybe I need a cold shower to get my mind in right order.*

Cam walked toward his pond. He bent down and picked up a rock, then skipped it across the water. He'd done it earlier in the day as well. Sadie's face had brightened when the pebble bounced several times on top of the water. For a gal who'd lived around the Smoky Mountains for several years, she didn't know very much about nature. Her unsuccessful efforts to skip a rock had made him laugh. Even now, the memory brought a smile to his lips.

He scratched his jaw to clear his mind. Even if he wasn't being unfaithful to Brenda, Sadie was too young for him. He was thirty-four, nearly thirty-five. Sadie was a full ten years younger than he was. An entire decade. Why, when he was a senior in high school, she would have only been in second grade. He snarled. The thought was disgusting.

But you're not in high school, are you? Nor is she in second grade.

He sighed at the inner nudging of his heart. In truth, ten years probably wasn't too much time since they were both adults. She'd experienced as many challenges in her life as he had in his. Of course, hers were different, but they were no less difficult. She'd graduated college; he'd never even attended. She'd had a child and given her up; he'd experienced the first five years of raising a child, but not a biological offspring.

Growling at where his thoughts were going, he shoved his hands in his pockets and stared into the night sky. Stars dotted the expanse, and as it had since he was a child, his gaze sought out the Big and Little Dippers. He thought of the third reason he didn't need to think of Sadie in such a way.

This reason had brought devastation to Brenda. As long as he lived, he would never forget the look in her eyes when they'd heard the news. She was committed to him, to their relationship, but her eyes tattled of a heart broken into a million pieces.

God, I could never do that to another woman. Never.

He turned and started back toward the house. *"For God is greater than our hearts, and he knows everything."* One of the many verses that Brenda had pasted around the house during her battle flooded his mind.

What do You mean, Lord?

A slight breeze brushed his face, and only the insects responded to his question. In his spirit, however, he knew. It had something to do with hurt and healing.

six

Sadie slipped into one of the available seats around the oversized, oblong meeting table. In a little over a month, she would begin working every day in her small office, reviewing and preparing files for the various students for whom she would provide services. She'd guide the special education teachers throughout the county in proper physical or mental exercises that would benefit students who were delayed or injured in some way. She'd meet with parents, interview students, study their abilities, work to find their physical and mental boundaries, design activities to stretch them. She would celebrate with students, parents, and teachers as individual goals were met and exceeded. Though at times trying—she remembered the father she'd worked with the last school year—overall her job proved exceptionally satisfying.

Today, however, she'd have the opportunity to meet the principals, assistant principals, and counselors from each of the schools. Though she felt no small degree of trepidation, she'd looked forward to this day. Confident in her ability to get a good feel for a person quickly, she expected to leave with an idea of how to work and communicate effectively in each school.

Most of the chairs were already filled, and though she sat beside an older woman on her left and a middle-aged man on her right, neither opted to introduce themselves. Normally, Sadie would go ahead and do so herself, but already the atmosphere in the room had taken on a more professional, less friendly air than what she was accustomed to in North Carolina.

Don't worry. She inwardly discouraged the butterflies that had begun to flutter in her stomach. *By the end of this day, I will know everyone's name. The woman whose position I've acquired worked here for thirty years. I knew before I accepted the job I'd have big shoes to fill.*

Sadie forced a smile to her lips as she scanned the faces around the table. Most everyone was at least twenty years her senior. Of course, it made sense for principals and counselors to be the more experienced people in a school building, but she was used to working with at least assistant principals who were closer to her age.

Sadie found herself picking at her already-chewed nails. Again, she inwardly reprimanded herself for the atrocious habit. It made her hands appear a wreck, and it definitely wasn't sanitary.

More people had come in. Only one seat remained unfilled. She noted the superintendent had not arrived either. Just as she realized his absence, he walked in. A young man, much closer to Sadie's age, followed him and claimed the empty seat.

Relief flooded Sadie. At least one face seemed to be somewhat near her age range. She clasped her hands at the silliness of her unease. In North Carolina, her dearest mentor had been a woman at one of the elementary schools who'd been thirty years older than Sadie.

Maybe it's not their ages that have my stomach tied in knots. Though the superintendent had started to speak, Sadie looked around the table once more. It wasn't age difference; it was the way they held themselves, the expressions on their faces. They all appeared to be generally unhappy to be there.

Sadie let out a long, slow breath. She noticed the younger man who'd walked in with her new boss. He smiled at her, exposing straight, ultra-white teeth. *Wow. He could be in a teeth-whitening commercial.*

Sadie stopped herself from laughing out loud. She didn't have a single problem with people who whitened their teeth. One time she'd even bought some over-the-counter whitener, but it had made her teeth so sensitive she quit using the strips after only three days. Still, every time she saw someone with knock-you-down white teeth, she had this inner urge to tell them just how unnatural it looked.

Of course, some of her friends had coffee and tea stains lightened at the dentist's office, but apparently there were various shades of white from which a dentist could choose. Ultra-white would never be her choice.

Sadie clenched her hands together on top of the table. *What am I thinking? Whitened teeth? I need to pay attention to my boss.*

Determined to listen, she looked up at her superintendent. He pointed to a chart on the wall that showed the statistics of kids in the county with disabilities of various kinds. *It does seem odd that he didn't introduce me to these colleagues.*

She squelched the thought. Different people handled new employees differently. He would most likely introduce her to them when they had a break or at the end of the session.

She tried to focus anew on her boss's words. Her nerves were getting away with her, and she found herself scanning the faces around the table again. The young guy was already looking her direction. He lifted his eyebrows and slightly nodded.

Sadie acknowledged him with a grin. This time she noted

his hair was a shade of brown, but not as dark as Cam's. His eyes, from across the table, appeared to be a light shade of blue, a very pretty color, but they didn't seem to portray the kindness that Cam's did. The man didn't even have a hint of a five o' clock shadow, unlike Cam, whose beard transformed him into a grizzly bear before the day ended. Of course, it was only the beginning of the day.

Why am I comparing him to Cam?

The realization sent her head spinning. The last thing she needed to do right now was fall for Cam Reynolds. Her goal was to spend as much time as she could with Ellie, eventually gain her trust, tell her the truth, and be the mother figure Ellie no longer had in her life. She did not need to start having feelings for a man who was still grieving his wife. For crying out loud, she was grieving his wife as well. In a different way, of course, but Sadie could honestly confess that she knew Ellie could not have been raised by a godlier, more loving, woman than Brenda.

God, I can't think about all this right now. Please help me focus on the superintendent. Picking up a pen, she looked back at her boss, determined to be able to relay everything he said, word for word.

◦ₐ

After two days of never-ending meetings with her new colleagues and never-ending inner battles about Cam Reynolds, Sadie was glad for the reprieve of spending a day with Ellie. Of course, Cam joined them, so she still had to fight her unyielding attraction; but at least she didn't have to try to keep her mind focused on the words of her superintendent. Sadie had at least been able to make her acquaintance with the others. As she feared, most of her colleagues had shared a close relationship with the past occupational therapist. She knew it would take time to gain their trust, and she was confident God would help her do so.

Sadie held Ellie's hand as they walked toward the breathtakingly gorgeous and ostentatious Winterthur country estate. Her landlord had told her she would need to visit Brandywine Valley multiple times even to begin to get a glimpse of some of Delaware's rich heritage. "You won't find history anywhere else in the United States like you'll find in the country's first state," he'd boasted. Taking in only a portion of Winterthur's majesty, she believed him to be correct.

She drank in the pink, lavender, blue, and white flowers, clustered together in various places. She wasn't very good at remembering the names of flowers, but she did note the yellow and orange daylilies that proudly displayed their perfection with the other flowers. She felt as if she were part of a picture that a master artist had created. The only word she could conjure in her mind to describe it was *breathtaking*.

And the smells. Oh, she could wrap herself up in the array of fragrances around her. Her heart raced and she threw back her head for a long, luscious inhaling of the place. A woman could easily get caught up in the romance of it. Unintentionally, she looked at Cam, who had slipped Ellie's free hand in his own.

He is such a good dad. Sadie could easily picture him with a whole team of children racing around his feet. She wondered if his children would have the same cute dimple that he had in his chin. *Ah! I've got to stop thinking about him like that.*

Ellie's voice squeaked as they neared their destination, allowing Sadie to escape her thoughts. "We're almost to the Enchanted Woods!"

"Yes, we are." Still holding Ellie's hand, Sadie leaned over and gave her an Eskimo kiss. "You'll have to show me everything."

Sadie stood back up and smiled at Cam. She knew her

elation probably showed through her eyes. The kindness that always radiated from him encouraged her to feel at ease with expressing her excitement.

With Sadie and Cam still holding her hands, Ellie began to swing her arms back and forth. "Oh yes, I will show you the stones you can walk on, the bird's nest, the troll's bridge. I'll show you the tree house. . . ."

"What about Harvey?" Cam asked.

Sadie watched as Ellie scrunched her nose. She let out a long breath. "I guess I'll show her Harvey, too."

Cam released a hearty laugh. "You're willing to share Harvey? You won't even let me touch Harvey."

Ellie pursed her lips and scowled up at her father. "Daddy, you are a boy. You're not allowed to hug Harvey."

"Hmm. I think I need to know who this Harvey is if I'm going to be hugging him." Sadie looked from Cam to Ellie.

Ellie puffed out her chest. "He's a frog."

Sadie felt her mouth drop open. "A what?"

Cam roared with laughter. "Yep. That's right, Sadie. Ellie loves to drag me over here so she can visit a frog."

Ellie stomped her foot. "You don't laugh at me and Sadie, Daddy."

Cam released Ellie's hand and lifted both of his in surrender. "Okay. Okay."

He peered into Sadie's eyes. Laughter still danced in them, and Sadie found herself willing to hug a nasty old frog for him. *Not him. For Ellie. I'd hug the frog for Ellie.*

"The frog is really a fountain that sits on a rock. He's enchanted, like the frog prince." Cam winked, and Sadie thought her feet would collapse beneath her. "You hug him for good luck."

"Not for luck, Daddy." She put her hand on her hip. "Because we love him."

"You're right, Ellie." Sadie mimicked her daughter by putting her hand on her hip and frowning at Cam. "There's no such thing as luck. Only God's workings."

"Touché." He lifted an imaginary hat off his head and bowed. "I completely agree."

Sadie's heart swelled. Yes, they did agree. Unlike Ellie's biological father, Cam had a relationship with God, a true love for the Lord. *And of course, now I know that is the most important thing I would ever look for in a mate.*

She pushed the thought away, and yet she couldn't deny the quickening of her pulse.

❧

Cam snuck a peek at Sadie in the passenger seat as they drove out of Wilmington. Her head leaned against the window, her eyes closed. Unsure if she was actually asleep or simply resting, he didn't dare look at her for too long. *Better keep your eyes on the road anyway, Reynolds.*

He looked in the rearview mirror. Ellie was asleep in her child seat. It had been a wonderful day at Winterthur. He'd visited several times with Ellie over the last few years. Brenda had endured the trip one time, but the heat and enormity of the place had worn her out for several days after.

Today was a really good day. He remembered the bliss on Sadie's face as she and Ellie crossed the troll's bridge hand in hand. Ellie had been every bit as excited as Sadie. His heart had nearly lurched out of his chest when Sadie and Ellie sat across from each other at the Acorn Tearoom. Their resemblance was uncanny. Somehow, it seemed right for the two of them to be together.

"Good heavens." Sadie sat up. She rubbed her eyes then trailed her fingers through her hair. "I can't believe I fell asleep. The drive isn't even that far."

"Nope."

Sadie touched his arm. Pleasure coursed through his body. "How long was I out?" She turned in her seat and looked at Ellie. When she did, she released his arm, and he instantly missed the weight of her hand. "Guess I'm not the only one who's exhausted."

"Definitely not. We'll be back at my house in just a few minutes."

Sadie nodded then leaned her head back against the seat. "Thanks so much for including me, Cam."

"It was my pleasure."

She had no idea how much pleasure it was for him. She was vibrant and exciting. He'd never meet another woman who would love his daughter any more than Sadie. The truth of it sank into his gut, making him yearn for the freedom to care about her as more than Ellie's biological mother. He exhaled as he pulled into his driveway. He unbuckled his seat belt and looked back at Ellie. "I think that kid's down for the count." He dangled the keys in front of Sadie. "Would you mind opening the door for me?"

Sadie bit her bottom lip but didn't take the keys. She stared into his eyes for a moment. "Would you mind terribly if I carried her inside?"

Cam lifted his eyebrows. "No, but she is a bit heavy."

Love filled Sadie's eyes. "She won't be to me."

His heart raced at the intense expression on her face. She loved with fierceness, with passion. The knowledge of it scared him, and he looked away and nodded. He fumbled for the car's handle. Finding it, he pushed open the door. He willed his feet to steady as he made his way to the front door and unlocked it.

Within moments, Sadie was behind him with Ellie draped over her shoulder. He'd never witnessed a person so happy to carry the deadweight of a sleeping child. Opening the door for her, he nodded toward the end of the hall. "Last room on the right."

"Thank you, Cam." Sadie's voice was little more than a whisper and was filled with intensity and hope.

Cam followed her inside Ellie's bedroom. He opened the dresser and lifted a pink nightgown from inside it while Sadie laid Ellie on the bed. Cam watched as Sadie gently unbuckled Ellie's sandals then slipped them off her feet.

Ellie startled and her eyes opened, her gaze searching the room in panic. Sadie caressed his daughter's cheek. "Hush now, sweetie. You're okay. You're home. In your bed."

Ellie's small frame relaxed, and she nestled her cheek into Sadie's hand. Cam heard Sadie's light gasp. She turned and took the nightgown from his hand. Gingerly, she changed Ellie then tucked her into bed as if she'd done it every day of Ellie's life. Leaning over Ellie once more, Cam watched as Sadie barely kissed his daughter's forehead.

Sadie stood to her full height and gazed at his child for a moment. Then she covered her face with her hand as her chest heaved in a cry. Cam wrapped his arm around Sadie's shoulder. She fit perfectly. "Come on." He guided her out of the room, down the hall, and into the living area.

Sadie broke away from his grip. "I'm so sorry, Cam." She swiped unsuccessfully at the tears that streamed down her face. "I can't believe I got this upset. I'm so. . ." She covered her face again.

"Come here." He wrapped her small frame in his arms. Her sobs escalated. Her back heaved. All he could do was caress her soft hair. "It's okay."

"I'm so sorry, so. . ."

"Shh." He nestled her closer. "It's okay to cry."

For what seemed an eternity, Cam endured her tears without the ability to kiss them away. He endured the light scent of her hair without the ability to inhale his fill. He endured the softness of her skin without the ability to really touch.

Finally, she pulled away. Inhaling deeply, she wiped her face with the back of her hand. With a slight chuckle, she looked at the black that smeared the top of her fingers. "Well, I must look a fright."

"Not too bad." Cam didn't have the heart to tell her that black streaked across her forehead, nose, and cheeks. He couldn't tell her that her eyes were swollen and puffy and that her nose shone like Rudolph's at Christmas. Anyway, he thought she looked adorable.

"I'll try not to do this every time I see you."

Cam lifted his hand and willed his heart to slow to its regular pace. "Not a problem."

"When can I see Ellie again?"

Cam let out a long sigh and smacked his jaw. "I forgot to tell you."

Sadie furrowed her eyebrows. "Forgot to tell me what?"

"Ellie is going to stay with my parents in Florida for two weeks. We're leaving in two days."

Sadie's shoulders slumped. "You'll be gone, too?"

Cam's heart skipped at the idea that she would care if he would be gone as well. "I'm flying her down there, but I'm coming back."

"Oh." Sadie frowned.

Cam shifted his weight from one foot to the other. "I thought it might be for the best. The anniversary of Brenda's death is next Thursday. . . ."

Sadie looked up at him. True regret shadowed her face. "Cam, I'm sorry."

His emotions seemed heightened tonight, and he swallowed back a lump that formed in his throat. "Thanks. I wasn't sure when my parents offered, but then my sister, Kelly, and I figured it would do the kids good to get away during that time."

"I'd say you're right." Sadie wiped at her face once more. "Will you call me when she gets back?"

Cam nodded. "I will."

She turned and walked toward the door. Cam watched as Sadie made her way to her car. She looked at her reflection in the rearview mirror, and Cam watched as she gasped and quickly licked her fingers to wipe at the traces of makeup across her face.

He chuckled. Two weeks would be an awfully long time for him not to see Sadie.

seven

Four long days had passed since Sadie's trip to Winterthur with Cam and Ellie. She was amazed at all Delaware had to offer, as well as the natural beauty that filled the state. Contented warmth filled her when she thought of Ellie grabbing her hand and escorting her to Harvey. Allowing Sadie to hug the frog statue proved to be an enormous honor Ellie gave to Sadie.

Night and day, she'd been physically ill with the desire to see her little girl again. She'd tried to keep herself busy with the food pantry ministry at the church. She'd talked with Lisa on the phone a couple of times, but her friend was busy caring for the boys, unpacking, and visiting with Rick's family. Sadie had also enjoyed a nice lunch with one of the assistant principals. The woman talked nonstop about her youngest daughter getting ready to head to college in the fall, but at least the outing had filled part of one day. Despite all that, Sadie had watched the news and checked the Internet multiple times two days before—the day Cam and Ellie were scheduled to leave for Florida. No airline accidents had been reported that she could find. Everything in her wanted to call and confirm they'd arrived safely, but Sadie didn't want to push too hard or too fast. *Especially after I broke down on him the other night.*

She slumped at the remembrance of it. It had been a long time since she'd come so unglued. Not one to embarrass herself quickly or handle it well, Sadie had been horrified at her body's overwhelming response to tucking Ellie in bed. She'd missed so much.

And Cam. She inhaled deeply as the light musky scent of him washed over her anew. How perfectly she fit in his embrace. His chest and arms were strong around her. The caress of his hand against her hair had been so gentle. A shiver coursed through her, and she cleared her throat, demanding her mind to clear as well.

Determined to think of something else, she drove to the Concord Mall in hopes of finding a new devotional book. She found several, finally selecting one. Of course, she couldn't help but notice the devotionals dedicated to little girls. She lifted the bookstore bag higher onto her elbow. *I can just say it's a welcome-back gift to Ellie.*

Sadie approached the counter of the fast-food restaurant in the food court. She smiled at the teenager standing beside the register who appeared to have more metal in her mouth than she had teeth. Cringing at the frizzy, un-netted hair of the teenage cook, she focused on not thinking about whether or not the boy's hands were clean.

"What can I get you?" The girl tapped her fingers on the counter.

"I'll take a bacon cheeseburger, no onion, a medium fry, and a chocolate milkshake." She brushed away the notion that she was probably going to devour an entire day's worth of calories in one meal. *One fatty meal won't kill me.*

She paid the cashier, took her food and several packets of ketchup, and headed for one of the few empty tables she could find. She sat and closed her eyes for the briefest of moments. *Thank You, Lord, for this food. Please allow me to enjoy it, because it's probably apple slices and water for dinner tonight.* She might have to add a bit of peanut butter to the slices, and maybe have milk instead of water. A gal needed her nutrients after all.

Opening her eyes, she saw a familiar face sitting across from her. "I didn't want to disturb your prayer," Mr. Ultra-white Smile explained. He motioned around the food court. "You can see there're no empty tables." Sadie spied one off to her right. "I thought we could share lunch together. . .maybe get to know one another a bit before school starts."

Though it unnerved her that he'd watched her pray, Sadie agreed it would be great to get to know him before the school year started. "Sure." She extended her hand. "In case you forgot, I'm Sadie Ellis."

The man smiled, exposing the teeth that reminded her of small pieces of Chiclets gum. Truly, they were very nice, just so bright. He shook her hand. "Yes. I remembered your name. I'm Charles Mann."

"It's nice to meet you again." Sadie took a drink of her milkshake. "I don't remember which school you work at."

"I'm the assistant principal at the middle school." Charles took a bite from his fruit cup.

Sadie noticed the grilled chicken wrapped in a wheat tortilla and cup of fruit on his plate. His drink looked clear, probably water. The man probably thought her diet was atrocious. "Great. Is there anything special you could share with me? Any specific ways of doing things?"

Charles told her who the secretaries were and which ones handled different office duties. He shared the way the past occupational therapist had communicated with the school counselor and psychologist. He filled her in on a few students he knew she'd be working with. His information was invaluable, and Sadie listened attentively. By the time she'd finished her lunch, she knew she could go into the middle school with some ease.

She wadded up her cheeseburger wrapper, careful to keep from spilling any condiments on the plastic tray. "Thanks so much for all the information, Charles. You've been very helpful."

"You're more than welcome." He paused, and she noticed he looked at her left hand for the fourth time since he'd sat down. Her female intuition knew what was about to happen, and she was not prepared to consider going on a date with one of her brand-new colleagues. He started to open his mouth again.

Sadie jumped up, scooping her tray into her hand. "Well, Charles, it was very nice having lunch with you, but I've got to go."

"Well, I. . ."

She looked at her watch. Truth truly was going to save her. "I really have to go. I have an appointment in half an hour."

"Okay. I'll see you."

She raced out to the parking lot. "Thank You, Lord, for hair appointments."

❧

Cam wrapped his fingers around the cool glass. Condensation wet his hands, bringing some relief from the warm Florida air. His mother had learned to make some really good sweet tea since she'd moved south, and he enjoyed as much of it as he could when he visited. He watched as his nieces and Ellie splashed around in his parents' pool. In a bit, he'd probably join them. His ears just weren't quite ready this early in the morning for the squealing of four girls.

The back door opened, and Kelly slipped into the seat beside him on the patio. "I told Mom and Dad about Sadie."

Cam nodded. It wasn't something he intended to keep from them. He'd struggled with missing her so much he'd simply opted out of talking about it.

"Mom's getting ready to join us outside."

"And Dad?"

Kelly swatted the air. "You know Dad. He doesn't have much to say about anything. He's going fishing."

Cam laughed. It was true. Norm Reynolds didn't get overly concerned with the intricate happenings in his children's lives. He cared about them. He wanted to see them happy. He just didn't need to know all the details.

"I'm a simple man," he'd proclaim and point to his chest every time Cam's mother got upset that Norm didn't want to listen to something she'd have to say. It wasn't that his dad didn't care. He had been a rock for Cam when Brenda died, but Cam knew Sadie showing up would be out of his dad's realm of possible discussion topics.

"Well, there you are." Cam's mother, Anita, slipped into the empty chair beside Kelly.

Cam grinned. His mother was going to ease herself toward the topic. But her *easing* often took so long they never actually had a chance to get to the topic.

Kelly leaned back in her chair. "Mom, I already told him I told you."

Cam chuckled. His family was so predictable. Dad bails. Mom eases. Kelly gets right to the point. *I wonder what I do.*

"Fine. Fine." His mother shifted in her chair. "I just didn't want to make the boy uncomfortable." She reached over and took Cam's hand. "You know you can talk to me about anything, don't you?"

"Yes, Mom. And I'll be happy to tell you what's going on. It's really quite simple. Sadie, Ellie's birth mother, finished college a few years ago. Now she's gotten a job in Delaware and wants to have a relationship with Ellie."

He didn't go into the fact that she'd purposely moved to Delaware after she found out about Brenda's death. And he most certainly wasn't going to tell her that the thought of her was keeping him up at night.

Kelly smacked the table and clicked her tongue in sarcasm. "See there, Mom. Nothing to it."

"Oh dear." His mother picked at the paper towel in her hand. "Why?"

Cam furrowed his eyebrows. "Why what?"

"Why does she want to do that? She gave Ellie up."

Cam searched his mind for the right response. His mother had no idea how hard it was for Sadie to allow Ellie to be adopted. He hadn't fully realized it himself until the other day when she cried in his arms.

Brenda and Sadie had often corresponded through e-mail and phone calls while Sadie was pregnant, and Brenda thought highly of Sadie. Once Ellie was born, they seemed to distance themselves from each other, but Brenda still felt so highly of Sadie that she was willing to keep her updated as Ellie grew. "Mom, Sadie was young when Ellie was born. She didn't have any help. She was very selective in choosing Brenda and me. I believe she's always loved Ellie."

"Well, yes. That may be so, but she did give her up. She can't just decide five years later she wants to be a mom."

Cam looked from his mother to Kelly. The last time he and his sister had talked about Sadie was that day in his garage. He wasn't exactly sure how Kelly felt about the situation either. "I don't think it's like that exactly. Sadie is a Christian, Mom. She was when she made a mistake in college. If you met her and talked to her, you would be able to see that her motives seem pure."

His mother straightened her shoulders. "That's a wonderful idea. I'd like to meet her when we fly the kids back to Delaware."

Panic punched him in the gut. The last thing he wanted

was for his mom and dad to meet Sadie. Cam shook his head. "No, Mom. Ellie doesn't know who Sadie is yet. We're taking it slow."

His mom seemed to ponder his words. Cam looked at Kelly. He still couldn't decipher how she felt. Taking a long drink of his tea, he rested back against the seat.

"You know, Mom," Kelly began. She twisted the straw in her drink between her fingers. "It might be good for Ellie to get to know Sadie."

"But what if she decides to up and leave? Ellie's already dealt with the death of a good, caring mother."

"You're right." Cam scratched his jaw. "That was my biggest concern, too." His own word—*was*—smacked him in the face with full force. Ever since the other night when he'd held a sobbing Sadie in his arms, Cam knew in his spirit that Sadie wouldn't leave Ellie.

He grabbed his mother's hand in his own. "I've only seen Sadie and Ellie together a few times. The woman adores my little girl. She. . .loves her."

His mother looked over at the girls playing in the pool. She turned back toward Cam and sighed. "You're a great dad, Cam. And you've always been a great judge of character. I'll be praying for you." She grabbed his chin between her finger and thumb. "But what's this look in your eyes?"

"What?"

"Are you developing feelings for this woman?"

Cam's mouth dropped open. He scowled at his sister.

"Kelly!"

Her eyes widened and she lifted her hands in the air. "I didn't say anything."

"What?" his mother squawked. "You really do have feelings for the girl? I was teasing. Well, sort of anyway. I thought I saw a bit of something in your eyes," she blustered and stood to her feet. "I'm heading to my room right now. You're going to wear out my knees praying for you, son."

"Join the crowd, Mom. I've already got calluses on mine."

❧

Sadie hung up the phone. It was Father's Day, and though she'd sent a card, her spirit urged her to call her father. He'd grunted his thanks for the card then passed the phone over to her mother. The conversation was stilted, never venturing from work or the weather.

Our relationship was never great, Lord, but I wish it were better than this.

Once a year she saw her parents, who lived in the state of Washington. When she'd been offered an academic scholarship at the small college in North Carolina, it had been an easy decision to leave home. Sadie resented how her parents had thrown themselves into their work while she grew up. They claimed to be Christians, attending church every Sunday and Wednesday. Her mom served on several committees, as did her father. But somewhere there had always been a faulty connection when it came to expressing feelings.

Well, I sure fixed that my sophomore year of college. Nothing like your only daughter calling home to say she's pregnant and her boyfriend's run off. Sadie shook her head at her actions. She was smarter than that. She was more conscientious than that. *Lord, You were dwelling within my heart and I tainted Your temple with my foolishness.*

Tears pooled in her eyes. She walked into the bathroom, grabbed a tissue, and stared at her reflection. "You've forgiven me, Lord. I know that." She wiped the tears from her cheeks. "But the consequences remain."

Not Ellie. Oh, how she loved Ellie. How thankful she was

that Ellie was fearfully and wonderfully made within her womb.

But she could never again get her virginity back. And her aloof relationship with her parents had grown more distant. The truth of it weighed her heart and spirit. Guilt always seemed to knock at her heart's door, begging for entry. Some days, shame would sneak up on her and she could barely see.

"For God is greater than our hearts, and he knows everything."

It seemed such a strange verse that always leaped into her mind when she struggled with her sin, and yet the years had shown her the verse fit perfectly within her spirit. Her heart was overburdened with the remembrance of the sin. Shame and guilt would always threaten. But God was greater than her heart—her feelings. He knew about her sin. He knew the outcome of mercy—the birth of Ellie—that resulted from her sin. He was stronger than her guilt, greater than her shame, and He knew everything.

Thank You, dear Jesus, for reminding me.

eight

Cam shoved the tickets to the DuPont Theatre into the front pocket of his jeans. He'd delivered a piece of restored furniture to one of his regular clients only an hour before. Mrs. Lawley had insisted he take the tickets she couldn't use. "Surely, there's some young lady at your church you could take to the musical? The DuPont always puts on a splendid performance."

Mrs. Lawley meant well, but he wasn't the slightest bit interested in going to see an all-student performance of *Less Miserable* or whatever she'd called the show. She'd said it was some famous musical, but he'd never heard of it. But then, he wasn't exactly current on musicals either.

Besides, it had been only one year, to the day, since Brenda's death. The last thing he wanted to think about was a musical or dating. *Mrs. Lawley doesn't realize she picked the worst day of the year to give those to me.*

From the passenger's seat, Cam grabbed the bouquet of flowers he'd bought to put in front of Brenda's tombstone. Deep emotion welled within him. He remembered Brenda's short blond hair, her light blue eyes. She had the sweetest dimple in her left cheek when she smiled.

His mind traveled back to their morning ritual before Brenda was sick. Cam would shower, dress for work, and then walk into the kitchen. Every day, Brenda would be sitting at the kitchen table, mug filled with hot tea in her hands, her gaze focused on a devotional. She'd look up at him and smile then turn her attention back to the book.

It was daily things like that Cam found he missed the most. He missed her strands of hair that had fallen in the bathroom sink, the robe she left lying on the closet floor, her slippers that stayed by the back door. They were all things that made life normal with Brenda, things that weren't found around the house now.

It is better that Ellie isn't here. I need to do this alone.

He stepped out of his truck, shut the door, and then leaned against it. It had been only a month since he and Ellie visited Brenda's grave, but today seemed harder. Not only was it the anniversary of her death; it was the first time he'd come alone.

Sadie would have come with me.

He looked at the heavens and whispered, "Why would I even think like that, Lord?" Taking a woman he was attracted to on a visit to his wife's grave was ludicrous. It was wrong.

One of the last memories with his wife began to replay in his mind. "Cam, I want you to promise me something," Brenda had said.

Cam held her hand tight. "I'll promise you anything, Brenda."

Tears welled in her eyes. "Promise me that if God gives you another woman to love, someone who would be a good mom to Ellie, you'll accept her."

"What?"

He remembered the fury that erupted within him. How could she even talk like that? God was going to heal Brenda. He would never be able to love another woman. No one else would ever have the opportunity to be Ellie's mother.

"You're young." Brenda had lifted her hand to his cheek. Even now, he could almost feel the softness, and weakness, of it. "And I know you will always love me."

Cam pushed the memory away. The idea had been ridiculous to him. He loved Brenda. He still loved Brenda. And he would never betray her.

You're not betraying her. There is no sin in your feelings for Sadie.

He pushed away from his truck. He would not think about Sadie Ellis today. Trudging toward Brenda's tombstone, he noted the smattering of flowers, wreaths, and trinkets adorning several of the graves. He wondered at the people who'd put them there, knowing they came from spouses, children, parents, friends of the people they'd lost. Death was so hard.

Finally, Cam reached Brenda's place of rest. A wreath rested on her grave. Cam frowned. It had been months since anyone but he and Ellie brought flowers here. Some of Brenda's friends from church had, on occasion, but not for a while. Her parents lived out of state and had seemed to want almost nothing to do with him or Ellie since Brenda's death. *Surely, they would contact me if they drove up.*

But it was the one-year anniversary; it would make sense for someone to bring a token of remembrance today. He looked around the wreath to see if a card or name tag was attached. He couldn't find anything.

Through his peripheral vision, he glimpsed a woman with long brown hair walking away from another grave. She looked familiar, and he turned to get a full look at her. *Sadie?*

Before he had time to consider his actions, Cam walked to her. Her back was still to him when he asked, "Sadie, what are you doing here?"

She turned, gasped, and covered her chest with her hand. "You startled me." She let out a breath and brushed a strand of hair back with her fingers. "I. . .well, I came to visit Brenda's grave. You'd said. . .well, you'd said she died on this date, and

I guess I just wanted to say good-bye."

Shifting from one foot to the other, she looked down at her fingernails. She seemed to avoid making eye contact with him, and Cam gazed at the tombstone she had been looking at. "Do you know this person, too?"

"Oh no." She glanced up at him, made eye contact, and then looked away. "I just noticed his dates of birth and death. He was only a baby. I guess I was just thinking about his mother."

Cam studied Sadie.

"Look, I didn't mean to be here when you were here. I just. . .well, I didn't know about her death when it happened." She picked at one of her fingernails. "And I. . .well, I thought of her as a friend. But I don't want to impose. I'm sorry."

She turned away from him, but Cam grabbed her arm. "Hey, it's okay. A lot of people cared about Brenda."

The musical tickets seemed to poke into his leg. It was on the tip of his tongue to invite her to go with him. But he couldn't.

Not today.

Today, he had to focus on the wife he'd lost.

Sadie looked into Cam's eyes. He drank in the compassion he saw reflected there. "Thanks, Cam." She moved from his grip and walked away.

Cam turned and headed back to Brenda's grave. A war raged within him. His love for Brenda, his attraction to Sadie. Guilt at the feelings Sadie stirred, sorrow at the memories he carried for Brenda.

The leaves of the trees scattered around the cemetery and seemed to fold the land into their embrace. He spied an American holly tree and could almost hear Sadie's voice. "The American holly is Delaware's state tree." Ellie's response would be to scrunch her nose and wonder if she was no longer a bug or a fish but now a tree.

A quick grin bowed his lips at the thought. He peered down at Brenda's grave, and remorse swept through him. *How could I think like that today? What kind of man am I?*

"Why do you look for the living among the dead?"

Scratching his jaw, Cam frowned. "Why in the world would I think that?" The angels asked that question to the disciples when they couldn't find Jesus' body after the crucifixion and burial. *But Jesus was alive. He's our Savior. Brenda is in heaven with Christ. She's not going to rise from this grave.*

"Exactly. But Sadie is alive."

Cam shoved his hands in the pockets of his jeans. He shook his head. "No. I will not think like this. I love Brenda. I will always love Brenda."

"Remember your promise. And the one who asked you to make it."

Frustrated, Cam swiped his hand across his face. He squatted and touched Brenda's engraved name on the tombstone. He traced the words LOVING WIFE, ADORING MOTHER. He whispered, "I will always love you, Brenda. You made me promise to allow another woman into my heart. I thought it was crazy. How could I ever do that?"

He cupped his hand over his mouth and looked past the grave, past the cemetery. He spied a single red house sitting just beyond a clear blue pond. Landscaped trees and bushes lay peacefully in perfect position around the home. He looked back down at the tombstone. "And here I find myself falling for another woman."

He closed his eyes and lifted a silent plea to God for help. Looking back at her name, he sighed. "Thank you for your blessing, Brenda. I don't know if I could have ever overcome the shame of how I feel for Sadie."

"Shame is never from Me."

Knowing the Spirit's nudging was true, Cam stood and turned in the direction Sadie had gone. The corner of the tickets poked into his leg again. *If she hasn't left, I'll ask her.*

Cam quickly made his way past several graves and to the road that curved through the cemetery. Her car was there, and Sadie sat in the driver's seat. He picked up his pace. Her eyes were closed. He didn't want to scare her. "Hey." He announced his presence, and she looked over at him.

A slow smile bowed her lips. "Hi, Cam."

"Penny for your thoughts."

Sadie blew out her breath. "I was just asking God to comfort you. . .and Ellie. I don't know if she knows that today is the anniversary of Brenda's death, but just in case." Her hands clutched the steering wheel. "I know this is hard for her, too."

Cam adored her sweet, caring spirit. She seemed to understand how much Brenda meant to him and to Ellie, and she wasn't jealous of it. She wanted to carve her own place in Ellie's life without taking away from Brenda. His heart swelled. *Now's a good time to ask.*

He pulled the tickets out of his front pocket. "A client of mine gave me tickets to the DuPont Theatre."

He gripped them tighter in his hand. It had been years since he'd asked a woman on a date. *Is this really going to be a date?* His gut tightened, and his head started to thump. *Just ask her, Reynolds.*

"It's some musical put on by students. I was wondering if you'd like to go."

"As a date?"

Cam felt heat creep up his neck and cheeks. *She probably thinks I'm too old for her.* "I. . .well, we could always talk about when we'll tell Ellie."

Way to wimp out.

Sadie seemed to relax. "Sure. I would love to."

✤

I cannot believe I didn't even ask him which musical we're going to see. Sadie stepped into a black high-heeled sandal while she pushed the back of her diamond stud earring into place. She looked into the full-length mirror and twisted her hips, allowing the simple, knee-length black dress to flare. A black satin ribbon, tied in the front, gave the dress just enough pizzazz to make it appropriate for an evening out.

She'd debated on whether to wear her hair in a clip or allow it to hang free past her shoulders. The hairdresser had cut several layers into her long hair, and Sadie loved the way the first layer framed her chin, the second rested just below her shoulder, and the length of it finally ended at the middle of her chest. Since Cam had never seen her hair up, she'd decided to go ahead and use the clip. The choice accentuated the curve of her neck and shoulders.

I certainly look like a woman going on a date, not just spending a little time with the father of her daughter.

Rolling her eyes, she picked up her small black purse. "Every time I think that, it sounds so weird, even to my own ears."

Her doorbell rang. *There's Cam.*

She snuck one last peek in the mirror before she straightened her shoulders and headed to the front door. Sucking in her breath, she tried to plaster a how's-it-going-friend smile on her face. He'd made it perfectly clear he wasn't thinking of this as a date. The last thing she wanted to do was make him think she was hitting on him. She flung open the door. "Hi, Cam."

"Wow." His mouth popped open, and he stared at her.

Sadie could have responded the same way. Cam looked sensational in his dark khaki pants and pressed polo shirt. The deep green color of the shirt brought out the flecks of green in his hazel eyes. She took in his jaw and chin, shaved clean, and once again noticed his deep dimple. Without thinking, she poked it.

She sucked in her breath and pulled her hand back. Warm embarrassment washed over her. "I'm so sorry."

Cam laughed. "As scruffy as I usually look, you probably didn't know it was there."

Sadie shook her head. *What was I thinking?* "I can't believe I did that."

"Hey, it's nothing. Kids used to ask me all the time if someone poked my chin with a pencil." He offered her his elbow. "You ready?"

She nodded, slipping her hand into the crook of his arm. He smelled amazing. The light musky scent she remembered the night she'd cried in his embrace was stronger and fresher. If he'd belonged to her, she'd have leaned over, touched the side of his neck, and inhaled her fill of him. *But he isn't mine, and I would do good to remember that.*

"You look beautiful, Sadie."

Cam's voice was so close she could almost feel the softness of it. If she turned and tilted her head just a bit, she could kiss him.

"Thank you," she whispered, determined to keep her focus ahead. After what seemed an eternity, they made it to the passenger side of his truck. He opened the door and she slipped inside; then he walked over and jumped into the driver's seat. "I never asked, but what musical are we going to see?"

Cam scrunched his nose much like Ellie did, bringing a smile to Sadie's face. *She must have picked that up from him.* "It's some weird French name, *Less Miserable.*"

"*Les Misérables?*" She bit the inside of her lip.

"Is that bad? I've never heard of it. 'Course, I don't check out musicals very often. We don't have to go."

"Oh no. No. It's a wonderful story. You may love it."

"But you don't?"

Sadie contemplated her answer. "It's not that I don't like it. It's an amazing musical, full of emotion."

Cam cocked one eyebrow.

"The last time I saw it, I cried through the whole thing." Sadie spit the words out as fast as she could.

Cam grinned. "So we need to stop and get some tissues?"

She shrugged her shoulders. "Maybe."

Cam's laughter filled the cab of the truck. He turned the ignition and pulled out of the parking space. "The last time you used my shirt as a tissue."

Sadie ducked her head. "Sorry 'bout that."

"I didn't mind."

❧

Cam couldn't pay attention to the musical. He really didn't care much about it to begin with, but having Sadie beside him, smelling like a flower garden and looking like she'd stepped down from heaven, all the while sniffling and wiping her nose with a tissue, was more than he could handle. He'd been raised to protect women, especially the lady he loved, and right now, she sat beside him drenching yet another tissue with tears. *I'm not sure how her tear ducts keep up with all the leaking*.

He bit back a laugh at his thought. Sadie was without a doubt one of the most emotional women he'd ever met. He'd never seen anything like it, but it did explain why Ellie seemed so prone to tears and dramatics.

A soft sniffle sounded beside him, and Cam could take it no more. He gently lifted his arm around her, squeezing her shoulder with his hand. To his surprise, Sadie nestled closer to him and rested her head against his shoulder.

His breath caught at the nearness of her. Her scent grew stronger around him, and it would only take a slight turn of his head to kiss her head. Her soft hair caressed his neck, sending his nerve endings into overdrive. *Comforting her may not have been the wisest of ideas, Reynolds.*

He swallowed back his desire to draw her closer to him, to tilt her head, take her face into his hands, and claim her lips against his own. *Lord, give me strength,* he inwardly begged, knowing it would take God's intervention to keep him from blurting out his feelings for her.

Again, he tried to focus on the musical. His awakened senses at Sadie's nearness had kept him from watching a large portion of it. He had no idea where the plot was going, and in truth, he didn't care. He only wished the thing would end so that he could release Sadie's shoulder and then get some fresh air.

Finally, the musical ended and Sadie looked up at him. She hadn't sat up and Cam found his lips mere inches from hers. "Thanks for holding me."

Her words were soft, her gaze filled with emotion—from the play, he forced himself to believe. And yet she seemed to search him as well.

"You're welcome." Cam's voice was rough and low. He swallowed back his desire to kiss her. Sadie seemed to hesitate before she moved away from him. Cam couldn't help but wonder if she yearned for a kiss as well.

Cam shook his head. He wasn't ready to think that way. Brenda may have given her blessing for him to find another wife, but Cam hadn't agreed. He never would have imagined himself with someone like Sadie, and he had no intention of imagining it now. *I'm just feeling weak because of the anniversary of Brenda's death. I don't really have feelings for Sadie.*

Cam stood and offered Sadie his arm. Her nails scratched gently against his skin, sending shivers up and down his arm. *Sure. You just keep telling yourself that, Reynolds.*

nine

Two weeks without Ellie had been hard on Cam. With her trip over and his parents back in Florida, Cam was glad to be tucking his little girl into her own bed again. He kissed the top of her head. She sat up and wrapped him in yet another hug. "I missed you, Daddy."

"I missed you, too, pun'kin."

Ellie released his neck and lay back on the bed. She nestled her special blanket close to her cheek. "I missed Sadie, too."

Cam nodded. "I bet she missed you as well."

"Daddy"—Ellie pulled the covers up to her chin—"is Sadie your girlfriend?"

Cam furrowed his eyebrows. "Why would you ask that?"

"Zoey said that she must be your girlfriend since you bring her with us to places. She said. . ." Ellie sat up, scrunched up her face, and twisted her shoulders back and forth. Her voice took on a sarcastic tone. " 'Ellie, why would Sadie want to be *your* friend?' "

Cam shook his head and ruffled her hair as she nestled back under the sheets. "Of course Sadie would want to be your friend."

"Zoey's a meanie."

"Hmm." Cam couldn't think of a good response. Zoey had changed so much since Tim's death. She looked for the bad in people and said so many things she shouldn't. The fifteen-year-old had his sister at her wit's end.

"So is Sadie your girlfriend?"

"No."

"Does she still want to be my friend?"

"Absolutely." Cam leaned over and kissed Ellie's head a second time. "Now go to sleep."

He reached for her pink lamp with the feather shade and turned off the light. Ruffling her hair one last time, he knew he had to call Sadie. It didn't surprise him that Kelly's girls would think that Sadie was his girlfriend. Why else would a woman just start hanging out with him and Ellie?

Walking out of the room, he asked God to give him and Sadie wisdom for how to tell Ellie the truth. After fishing her phone number out of his wallet, Cam picked up the phone and dialed her number. A ring sounded in his ear. *Oh God, what will she say when I tell her? How will I tell her?* If he were honest with the lot of them, he would announce to the whole family that he'd like nothing more than to make Sadie his girlfriend.

He growled as another ring sounded through the phone line. *You know better than to think that way, Reynolds.*

"Hello?" His heart stirred at the sound of her voice. It had been a week since their date to the musical. Neither of them would come out and say it was a real date, but for Cam it had been nothing less. "Hi, Sadie. How have you been?"

"I'm good." She hesitated. Cam detected the uncertainty and hope in her voice. "Is Ellie home?"

"She is." Cam tried to keep his tone light. He wasn't sure if Sadie was ready to fess up to her true identity. He wasn't sure he was ready, but he didn't see they had any other choice. "I need to talk to you about that."

"Okay." Her voice sounded meek, almost scared.

"Well, when I put her to bed, she told me that—"

"Oh, Cam, please don't say I can't see Ellie anymore." Her words came out fast, choppy, and filled to the brim with emotion. He could picture her eyes pooling with tears.

Cam frowned. "No. I wasn't going to say that. God's given me peace about you being in Ellie's life." He furrowed his eyebrows as he sought for the right words. "I think you're good for Ellie. She needs you."

I'm finding I need you, too. He shook his head at the thought. Focused. He had to stay focused.

"Thank you, Cam. I love her so much. I love getting to see her." She paused, and Cam knew she wiped tears from her eyes. The woman cried at the drop of a hat, and he adored her for it.

"We're going to have to tell her the truth," Cam blurted out before she could make more assumptions. "I know we were going to talk about it the night of the musical, but. . ."

"Okay." Silence filtered through the phone. "Are we ready for that?"

Cam walked into the living area and spied Ellie's snack dishes on one of the end tables. He rested the phone between his shoulder and ear so he could pick up the glass and plate. "I don't think we have a choice." He made his way back to the kitchen, rinsed the dishes, and placed them in the dishwasher. "Kelly's kids think you're my girlfriend."

"What?"

"Kelly's oldest told Ellie that you must be my girlfriend or why else would you be hanging around."

Sadie didn't respond for several moments. Part of Cam just wanted to tell her that he was all right with that assumption. If she didn't have a problem with the ten-year age difference, then he was ready to make it truth. If he hadn't seen her at the cemetery and then taken her to the DuPont Theatre, he didn't think he would have made it without seeing her the full two weeks Ellie was gone.

"Okay. When?" Uncertainty sounded from Sadie's voice.

Cam scratched his chin. "Tomorrow's a Saturday. If you're available, how 'bout we take her to the Brandywine Zoo tomorrow? We can tell her then."

"Okay. I'll be at your house at ten." She paused again. "Cam, can we tell her before we go? I want to be able to answer any of her questions. She has to know how much I loved her."

Cam smiled into the phone. There was no way Ellie, or anyone, could doubt Sadie's love for his daughter. "Sounds great. And, Sadie, don't worry. Ellie knows you love her. She loves you."

⁂

Praise music blared through the car's radio as Sadie drove the road to Cam's house the next morning. Sadie had not slept a single moment since her phone conversation with Cam. She'd tossed and turned, lifted the covers higher under her chin, pushed them off, turned on the fan, turned off the fan. She'd read scripture, which helped some, but she could not hand her fear of Ellie's reaction completely over to God. What if her child never wanted to see her again?

Peeking in the rearview mirror, Sadie noted how puffy her eyes looked from her restless night. She glanced back at the road, screamed, and swerved, barely missing a squirrel. Placing one hand on her chest, she blew out several breaths. Every fiber of her body, inside and out, seemed to shake uncontrollably.

"Calm down, child. Doesn't My Word say 'the truth will set you free'?"

"Yes, Lord. I have to trust You. She needs to know the truth."

Sadie pulled into Cam's driveway, parked, then walked to the front door. Before she had a chance to knock, Cam opened the door and wrapped her in a bear hug. Momentarily taken aback, Sadie stood still with her arms stiff at her sides. Cam whispered, "It'll be okay."

Tension that seemed to have locked her joints and muscles released at his words and touch, and Sadie found herself wrapping her arms around Cam. He felt strong and secure. A wave of knowing she could face anything with him overwhelmed her. *How can I be falling for this man?*

She didn't know why. She simply knew she was. This embrace, so similar to the last one they'd shared, was Cam's way of calming her. This time she wasn't overwrought with sobs and sadness at the things she'd missed. This time her senses were very much awake and alive and sensitive to every inch of him embracing her. His breath warmed her scalp, and she feared she'd melt at the heat of it.

His hand cupped the back of her head. His lips brushed against her forehead. Then he moved his mouth down toward her ear and whispered, "I'll be right here."

He pulled from their embrace but kept one hand on her arm. She looked up into his eyes. *Wow! What this man does to me! I want so much to tell him how I feel. Why? Why can't I tell him?*

"Sadie!" Ellie's squeals of delight interrupted Sadie's thoughts. Ellie raced toward Sadie, and Sadie lifted her daughter off the ground and spun her around.

"I missed you so much." Sadie gave her little girl an Eskimo kiss.

"I missed you, too." She twirled a lock of Sadie's hair between her fingers. "Daddy says we're going to the zoo today. I'm going to show you the alligators."

"I can't wait." Sadie, still holding Ellie, walked into the living room and sat on the couch. "Your daddy and I want to talk to you first."

"But I'm ready." Ellie stuck out her bottom lip. "Daddy's

already fixed my hair." She lifted her foot. "And I put on my sandals."

Sadie bit back a grin. She didn't know how she'd ever manage disciplining Ellie. Even her whining was so cute. *One day soon, I'll have no choice.* "I know, honey, but this is important."

Cam sat on the chair across from them. He leaned forward, clasping his hands between his legs. "Ellie, remember how I told you that Mommy and I picked you out special, just for us?"

Ellie nodded.

"Remember we told you that you were adopted?"

Ellie nodded again before scrunching her nose. "I can't remember what *adopted* means."

Sadie trailed the length of Ellie's hair with her fingers. She fought back the urge to squeeze her tighter into her lap for fear the child might leap away when she found out who Sadie really was.

Cam continued. "*Adopted* means that a different man and woman gave birth to you, but your mommy and I raised you."

"I don't get it."

Sadie smiled at Ellie's response. "How about this. Ellie, do you know anybody whose mommy had a baby?"

Ellie smiled. "Trudy's mommy had a baby."

"Did her tummy get really big?"

Ellie nodded. "Yep. That was the baby inside her belly. Trudy said the baby has to grow up a lot before he could be born."

Sadie nodded. "That's right. You had to grow up in somebody's belly."

"Yep. I grew up in Mommy's belly."

Sadie swallowed. Now was the time to tell her. "Well, actually. . ." Sadie gazed into Ellie's eyes, so innocent, so trustworthy. "You grew up in my belly."

Ellie scrunched her nose and frowned. Sadie compared a strand of Ellie's hair to hers.

"See how our hair looks alike?" She poked Ellie's nose. "And you have my nose?"

"But. . ." Ellie blinked several times. "Trudy's mommy is the baby's mommy. You're not my mommy."

Sadie's heart clenched. An expression that Sadie recognized from five years before covered Ellie's face. It was the same look of confusion and wonder that Ellie had when the doctor laid her on Sadie's chest before taking her to Cam and Brenda. *I am your mommy, Ellie. I am, just like Brenda was.*

Cam picked up the family picture that sat on the end table beside him. "Ellie, this is your mommy. Brenda was your mommy, because she adopted you." He touched Sadie's arm. "Sadie is the mommy who gave birth to you. She carried you in her tummy."

Ellie studied Sadie for several painstaking moments. Sadie wished she could plunge into Ellie's mind and discover all the thoughts and feelings that were going on inside. She wanted the opportunity to ensure every fiber of Ellie's being that she had always loved the little girl. Always.

Suddenly, Ellie's eyes widened and she touched Sadie's cheek. "Can I call you '*Mommy*,' too?"

❧

A few hours later, Cam followed Sadie and Ellie as they walked hand in hand toward the lions' cage at the zoo. He was still in shock that Ellie wanted to call Sadie "Mommy." He'd expected her to handle it well. Even though she didn't fully understand adoption, he and Brenda had always told Ellie she was adopted.

At the same time, he hadn't expected her to replace Brenda in her mind so quickly. *Maybe* replace *isn't the right word.* He raked his fingers through his hair. *What is the right word?*

He watched as Sadie picked up Ellie and placed the child on her hip. Ellie was too old to be held, but he was guilty of the same gesture. Ellie'd had to deal with so much in her life that Cam often found himself babying her. Sadie would want to baby her because she'd never had the opportunity before now.

- Brenda had been so sick for almost half of Ellie's life. Ellie had often been taken to a friend's, a church member's, or the babysitter's house when Brenda wasn't well. Everyone doted on his little daughter. As a result, she loved to go places and visit people. *Maybe that's why she's so quick to call Sadie "Mommy."*

And Sadie would be a good mommy for Ellie. There was no denying it. He watched as Sadie pointed to one of the monkeys in the far right corner picking bugs from its head and eating them. Ellie's laugh filled the air.

Though part of him felt sadness for Ellie's quick acceptance of Sadie, the other part of him praised God for it. With Cam's feelings growing each passing day, it made the possibility of dating Sadie much easier to consider.

He'd felt such peace at the cemetery about being able to let Brenda go. Maybe this was God's sign that Ellie would be ready, too.

He smiled at the thought of it. Walking up behind them, he touched Ellie's hand. "Are you ready for some lunch?"

Ellie nodded. "Uh-huh. I'm starving."

Sadie put Ellie down and grabbed her hand. "Well, then let's go eat."

"Okay, Mommy." Ellie reached up with her free hand and grabbed Cam's. "Let's go, Daddy."

Cam peered over at Sadie. Her bottom lip quivered, and he knew each time Ellie said the endearment, Sadie nearly came unglued.

They made their way to the nearest food vendor. After ordering hamburgers and fries, the three sat at an open table. While Cam opened a ketchup packet for Ellie, Sadie wiped his daughter's hands with a wet wipe.

"Your daughter is beautiful." An elderly woman stopped beside their table.

Cam and Sadie looked up and then at each other. Cam watched as Sadie's eyes widened in surprise. He winked then looked up at the woman. "Thank you."

"She's as pretty as your wife."

He glanced at Sadie, whose face and neck burned red. "Well, she's not my—"

The woman continued, "My own children were about five years apart. I had three boys." She looked from Cam to Sadie. "Are you planning to have more children?"

Sadie dropped the wet wipe in a glob of ketchup. "Oh my." She picked it up and tried to wrap the clean part around the soiled.

"We haven't really talked about it." Cam wasn't really lying. Yes, he knew the woman believed them to be married, but they *hadn't* talked about more children.

Sadie's mouth dropped open, and her cheeks blazed.

"Wouldn't you like a little brother or sister?" The woman bent down and pinched Ellie's cheek.

Ellie looked up for the first time. She turned to look at Cam and then Sadie. "I can have a baby brother or sister?"

"Well—" Cam touched Ellie's hand. *Okay, now the conversation is getting out of control.*

"I want a baby brother like Trudy has. Then I can feed him and change his diaper. . . ."

A man called from several tables over. The elderly woman waved then peered back down at them. "I'd better be going.

My husband has our food." She pinched Ellie's cheek one more time. "You are a little cutie. Bye, now."

"Bye," Cam and Sadie both mumbled over Ellie's chattering. She was still going on about the many things she could do with a baby brother.

Cam peeked over at Sadie, who looked as if she would pass out at any moment. "That was interesting." He dropped several fries in ketchup then shoved them in his mouth.

"To say the least." Sadie took a sip of her soft drink.

"Mommy?" Ellie sat on her knees in her seat to get her face closer to Sadie's. "Do you want to have a baby brother?"

Sadie swallowed. She gazed over Ellie's head and into Cam's eyes. "Only God knows how many children someone will have."

"But do you want one?" Ellie implored.

Sadie's gaze never left his. Her light green eyes seemed to probe him with questions and desires. Cam found himself crushing the napkin in his hand from the intensity of it. "Yes. I want as many babies as God will give me."

She smiled, and Cam knew to the depth of his being that Sadie returned his feelings for her. Her answer was meant for him.

And now that he knew it, he had to let her go.

ten

The month of July and the first part of August passed too quickly for Sadie. She'd taken every opportunity she could to spend time with Ellie. They'd swum at the pool, played at the park, eaten lunch at every fast-food restaurant they could find. Sadie couldn't get enough of spending time with her little girl. She longed to ask Cam if Ellie could spend the night with her sometime, but she hadn't quite gotten up the nerve.

Besides, something has changed about Cam. For a while, Sadie had been convinced that Cam had feelings for her. Though taken aback at the attraction she felt for Cam, over time she'd warmed to the notion and started to hope that God would allow something to flourish.

Sadie carried a box of file folders, papers, and personal items into the small office the school board had given her at the county's central office. After dropping the box on the desk, she smacked her hands together then wiped them on her shorts. She swiped the small beads of sweat that had formed on her forehead with the back of her hand.

But boy, was I wrong about Cam having feelings for me. Sure, he'd been nice to her, allowing her to see Ellie pretty much when she wanted. He still went with them on a few of the excursions. But *nice* was the only word she could use to describe Cam. He didn't hug her. He didn't look at her. He didn't talk except when necessary.

Sadie had no idea what had happened. *Surely, he felt something those times he hugged me.* Shivers raced up and down Sadie's spine as she reminisced the times. She still felt something from them. Her attraction to Cam hadn't diminished a bit.

She remembered the time Ellie had fallen and badly scraped her knee at the pool. Sadie had raced to the concession stand for an adhesive bandage and ointment. When she returned, Cam held a whimpering Ellie in his lap, rocking her back and forth. He took the first-aid material from her and within moments had bandaged the wound and carried her to the concession stand for a Popsicle. The man loved Ellie with all that was in him.

Sadie wanted that for herself as well.

I need to get back to work. All this stewing about Cam isn't going to change the way he feels about me.

Sadie opened the file cabinet and thumbed through the names of the students she would be working with. The woman before her had been meticulous in her filing method. Everything was in order and color-coded with all documentation completed. "It's no wonder they all loved her. I love her myself."

"Well, hello there." Sadie looked up to find Charles Mann, the middle school assistant principal, leaning against the door frame, his smile brightening her room. He crossed his arms in front of his chest. "So are you ready to start?"

"I sure am." Sadie shuffled two of the files on her desk. She liked Charles just fine. He seemed to be a great guy, but she simply wasn't interested. However, each time she saw him, she couldn't help but think the feeling wasn't mutual.

"How long have you been here today?"

Sadie looked at her watch and gasped at the late hour. "Almost eight hours! It's nearly four o'clock." She thought of the peanut butter crackers and soft drink she'd swallowed down several hours before. *That's why I'm getting so hungry.*

Charles chuckled. "You've put in a long day. Why don't you

let me take you to dinner?"

"I'm sorry. I can't. I have kindergarten orientation tonight."

Charles frowned. "They require you to go to kindergarten orientation?"

Sadie chuckled. "No."

She watched as he looked at her ring finger then back up at her face. "Do you have a child in kindergarten?"

"Well, I. . ."

Charles's cell phone rang. He looked at the number. "I'm sorry. I have to take this. I'll talk to you later."

Sadie sighed in relief as he walked down the hall. She realized again how difficult it would be to explain her relationship with Cam and Ellie to other people. She'd been so worried about Ellie's response to her that she hadn't considered others. Many of the people at church now knew and for the most part had accepted her. She'd become so involved with the children's ministry, the food pantry, and Sunday school that many of the parishioners had been able to get acquainted with her as a person as well as her as Ellie's biological mom. The memory of telling Kelly and her girls permeated her mind. Kelly already knew and seemed happy for Sadie to be a part of Ellie's life. It had been wonderful to meet her.

But her girls, especially her oldest daughter, were another story. The youngest one's expression only showed her disbelief and uncertainty. The middle daughter was quiet, retreating to her room. But the oldest was quite vocal. She hadn't held back her thoughts on the situation. "It's not right for her to come here," the girl had argued with Cam. "She gave Ellie up. She didn't want her. How could you do that to Aunt Brenda?"

Though Kelly had reprimanded and grounded the girl and made her apologize, Sadie was haunted by the teenager's words. She wondered how many people would feel as Kelly's daughter did. *They just probably won't be as vocal to my face.*

With anxiety about the kindergarten orientation mounting within her, Sadie placed the folders back in the file cabinet. She locked her door and headed out into the parking lot. In a little over an hour, she was going to meet Cam and Ellie at a restaurant for dinner before they headed to the school. She needed to talk to Cam in private before that. After pulling her cell phone from her purse, she dialed his number. His answering machine picked up. "Cam, I hope you check this. I'm going to come over before we head to the restaurant. We need to talk."

❧

"What could she possibly need to talk about?" Cam mumbled as he lathered his face with shaving cream. He hadn't shaved in a few days, and he knew this was going to hurt. He could thank his father for his hairy genes.

"Daddy, I put on my dress that Mommy bought me," Ellie called from the other room.

Cam moved the razor down his jaw then rinsed it in the sink. "Okay, pun'kin." The girl wore that dress every day she could. This weekend, Cam planned to ask Sadie to go with them to buy school clothes. If Ellie thought Sadie picked them out, he knew Ellie would want to wear them.

After finishing his shave, he patted his face with a warm towel. He heard the front door open, and Sadie's voice filtered through to his bathroom. He glanced at the clock on his bedroom dresser. *She's an hour early.*

Inwardly, he groaned. It had been hard enough trying to avoid looking at her when they had lots of activity planned. Having her in his house for a full hour of talking would unravel him. His attraction intensified with each moment they spent together. But he couldn't have her.

The ten-year age difference he'd been worried about in the beginning was nothing. He'd even come to accept Brenda's blessing to allow a new wife, and Sadie would fit perfectly into his and Brenda's hopes for a mother for Ellie. But having more children. . . There was no getting past the difficulty *that* caused.

He tossed the towel in the hamper and walked into the living room. Sadie sat on the couch with Ellie sitting on the floor between her legs. Sadie was fixing Ellie's hair in some sort of fancy knots down the back of her head. Sadie looked up at him and smiled. "Hey."

Cam's heart thumped beneath his chest. He wanted this woman. She looked right sitting on his couch, fixing their daughter's hair. *Our daughter.* What an irony that Ellie truly was the daughter of both of them.

Sadie twisted the ponytail holder in Ellie's hair. "Now go get a ribbon from your box that matches the dress."

"Okay, Mommy." Ellie skipped out of the room.

Sadie leaned forward. "We need to talk while she's gone."

"Okay."

"What are we going to tell her teacher?"

"About?"

She pointed at herself and then at him. "About us."

Cam's pulse quickened, and he slowly sat in the chair across from Sadie. She had no idea how much he wanted an "us" between them. Not only was Sadie one of the most beautiful women he'd ever known; she was a wonderful mother with a sweet, giving nature, and she loved the Lord. She was perfect for him. But he could never be perfect for her. He gripped the arm of his chair. "What about us?"

Sadie shook her head. "Really, I guess I mean *me*. What are we going to tell her teacher about me?"

"That you're her mom."

"What about you?"

"I'm her dad."

"But what if she asks if we're divorced? Is this going to be hard for Ellie? I wanted to be in Ellie's life so badly." Sadie wrung her hands. "I never thought about what other people would think or say. Remember your niece's reaction."

Cam frowned at the memory of Zoey's complete disrespect. In truth, he hadn't thought much about the reaction of other people until then either, but he didn't think a teacher would behave as badly as Zoey. And why would they have to tell her anyway? "Sadie, I really don't think a teacher's going to come out and ask if we're divorced." He nodded. "I know she'll probably assume it, but is it necessary to tell her the whole situation?"

"I don't know." Sadie raked her hand through her hair. "Is it?"

"No, I don't think so." Cam looked out the French doors that led to the backyard. He watched several ducks swimming leisurely on his pond. He looked back at Sadie. "If you're uncomfortable, you don't have to go tonight."

Sadie's lip puckered, much like Ellie's did when she was upset. The expression tugged at Cam's heart. "But I want to go."

"You know what? We don't have to tell her anything. You're Ellie's emergency contact number. For all she'll know, you're Ellie's aunt or cousin."

"I don't know."

Sadie's worried expression drew him. He wanted to slip onto the couch beside her, wrap her in a hug, and assure her all would be fine. But he didn't. He couldn't risk his emotions growing any stronger. *Who am I kidding? They couldn't possibly get any stronger. I know I love this woman.*

"I could just tell the truth." Sadie's voice was low. "Jesus told us 'the truth will set you free,' and it did when we told Ellie."

Cam shrugged. "I really don't think it will even come up."

❧

The kindergarten room was everything Sadie would have expected. The names of the students were printed in perfect handwriting on multicolored kites taped to the front door. A huge "welcome tree," filled with colorful leaves and birds, greeted them as they walked through the door. Small red tables with two yellow and two blue chairs each were placed strategically around the room. One corner contained a "reading" carpet. Another corner was designated for crafts. Six computer desks were lined up against one wall. Bright numbers and letters filled the walls, even hung from the ceiling. It was a beginning-of-education dream, and Sadie could hardly wait for Ellie to experience all of it.

A tall young woman walked up, her thin hand extended to them. Blond tendrils escaped the clip that held back her long hair. Her eyes, the bluest Sadie had ever seen, shone with warmth and excitement, and Sadie couldn't help but wonder if it was her first year of teaching. "Hi. I'm Miss Montgomery." She shook Cam's hand and then Sadie's. She leaned down and took Ellie's hand in her grasp. "Welcome to your classroom. What's your name?"

Ellie lowered her chin and clamped her lips together. She grabbed Sadie's hand, gripping it with all her strength. It was the first time Sadie had ever seen Ellie respond bashfully.

"It's okay if you're nervous, sweetie. We all get nervous sometimes," Miss Montgomery crooned. She touched the ladybug on Ellie's dress. "I like ladybugs. Did you know they're the state bug?"

Sadie bit her lip. She heard Cam bite back a grunt. Ellie

glanced up at Cam. "Why does everyone think we're bugs, Daddy?"

Cam howled, and Sadie couldn't hold back her chuckle. Confusion crossed the teacher's expression. Sadie put her hand on Miss Montgomery's shoulder. "I'm sorry. We've been learning about the state's symbols, and Ellie hasn't quite gotten to the point where she understands the concept."

Miss Montgomery smiled. "So your name is Ellie. You must be Ellie Reynolds. Did you see your name on the front door?" When Ellie shook her head, the teacher grabbed her hand. "Let's see if we can find it."

Sadie watched as Ellie and her teacher sought out and found Ellie's name. Miss Montgomery took time to show Ellie where her seat and cubby would be, as well as some of the daily activities she could expect. The whole time, the teacher made sure Cam and Sadie understood all that was expected. *There's no way this woman could be a first-year teacher. She intrinsically knows so much.*

"Ellie, why don't you color that sheet of paper sitting on your desk while I talk with your mom and dad? It will be your first kindergarten assignment," Miss Montgomery said.

"Okay." Ellie's face split with a smile. "I'll stay in the lines, too."

"That's wonderful." The teacher turned toward Cam and Sadie. "Were you able to complete the information packet I sent to you?"

"Yes." Cam handed her the packet.

She pointed toward the small chairs at an available table. "I know they're small, but if you'd like to have a seat, I'll make sure I have all the information I need." She opened the packet and skimmed the papers. She looked at Sadie. "You're Sadie Ellis?"

Sadie swallowed hard. She twisted her purse strap between her fingers. *She wonders why my last name is different. She's going to ask. Lord, what will I say to her?* "Yes."

"Are you our new occupational therapist?"

Sadie exhaled a long breath. "Yes."

"It's so nice to meet you. I hope you like it here."

Sadie's nerves started to settle. "I think I will. Thank you."

Miss Montgomery looked back at the papers, then back up at Cam and Sadie. "You're listed as her emergency contact number, but I like for that person to be someone who isn't in the home."

"I'm not in the home."

"Oh, I'm sorry." Miss Montgomery pointed to the paper. "I see here you have a different address. You must be divorced."

"No. Not divorced. We were never married."

Miss Montgomery's eyebrows furrowed into a straight line.

"I mean. . .we. . ." Sadie felt heat rush up her neck and cheeks.

The teacher shook her head. "It's okay. You don't have to explain."

"No, but I don't want you to think. . ." Sadie's heart sped. Panic pulsed through her veins. "Cam's her adopted dad. I'm her biological mom. You see, I was young when I found out I was pregnant, and then Cam's wife died, and I felt God was giving me the chance to see my daughter. . . ."

Beneath the table, Cam grabbed Sadie's hand and squeezed it. The warmth of his touch calmed her slightly, and she took a breath.

Miss Montgomery shook her head. "It's okay. Really. You didn't have to explain."

Sadie nodded. Embarrassment swelled within her, and she moved numbly through the rest of the meeting. Her mind reeled with worry. What if this young woman thought poorly of Ellie because of Sadie? Surely, she wouldn't. No one could fault Ellie. What if she talked with other teachers? Would they think negatively of their new occupational therapist? Bile rose in her throat. That was a real possibility.

eleven

"Mommy, this one is itchy." Cam watched as Ellie scrunched her nose and scratched at the back of the blue jean shorts. Sadie pulled the tag away from Ellie's skin and then buttoned the front. She slipped a hot pink shirt over Ellie's head. "I don't like it. It scratches my back." Ellie squirmed away from Sadie's grasp.

Cam bit back a chuckle. He rarely took Ellie shopping for this very reason. She whined. She complained. She got tired. It was easier to simply order stuff off the Internet and hope it would fit. Of course, they had been in the mall for three hours, and even the best of five-year-old shoppers would be getting tuckered out.

With the patience of an experienced mother, Sadie twirled Ellie to face her. "It only scratches because we can't take the tags off." She let out an exaggerated gasp as she turned Ellie toward the mirror. "Look at how pretty you are."

"I don't like it." Ellie puckered her lips.

"Hmm." Sadie cupped her chin with her thumb and finger. "I'll tell you what. As soon as we find one more outfit for you, we'll walk over to the pavilion and get some lunch. Would you like that?"

Ellie's eyes lit up. "I like this one." She started to unbutton the blue jeans. "Can we go eat now?"

"We sure can." Sadie helped her out of the new clothes and into the ones Ellie had worn to the store.

Cam scooped up the various shirts, pants, and dresses they'd selected and headed toward the register. "You know you're pretty good at this?"

"Pretty good at what?" Sadie pushed a strand of hair behind her ear—something about that always stirred Cam. Maybe it was the contour of her neck, or the slight, sweet whiff of her hair, or maybe he just wanted to be able to feel the softness of the lock.

Forcing his thoughts back, he laid the clothes on the counter then pulled out his wallet. "Taking Ellie shopping. You're very patient."

Sadie shrugged. "She's just a little girl, and we've been gone a long time. I know she's got to be tired—I'm exhausted."

Cam smiled as he paid for the clothes. Scooping up the bag with one hand, he grabbed Ellie's hand with the other. Sadie grabbed Ellie's free hand. They headed to the pavilion and—within minutes—sat at a table enjoying hamburgers, fries, and soft drinks.

Ellie seemed rejuvenated by the fatty meal and sugar rush. She talked incessantly about school and her new teacher. Sadie smiled and nodded, but Cam could see the hint of distress in her gaze. She'd gotten extremely nervous when they met Ellie's kindergarten teacher. Cam wondered if rumors were already flying about Sadie, the newcomer who'd given up a baby. People from all occupations could be cruel when it came to spreading gossip. Miss Montgomery seemed to be a wonderful woman, but he couldn't help but wonder if, and how, she would share the information Sadie gave.

"Well, hi, you guys."

Cam looked over to see Kelly and her youngest daughter standing beside their table.

"Hi, Aunt Kelly." Ellie jumped out of her seat and wrapped her arms around Kelly's waist. "I got new school clothes today."

Kelly looked at the bags on the floor. "It sure looks like it." She turned to Sadie. "Are you ready to start school?"

Sadie's distressed expression deepened, and Cam knew Sadie forced herself to smile. "I think so."

"Well, if you need anything, even if it's just someone to talk to, I'd be glad to listen. Remember, I'm at the high school. Junior and senior Language Arts."

Sadie tapped the side of her face. "That's right. I forgot you were a teacher." Her smile relaxed. "I appreciate the offer. I may have to take you up on that."

"You're the new girl, and some people can be. . .tough."

Cam noted the hesitancy in Kelly's voice. He wondered if rumors were already flying. Kelly looked at him, blinked, and then slightly nodded her head. Yep, the rumors were making their rounds. He'd given Kelly a heads-up about the kindergarten orientation, and Kelly was silently letting him know that Sadie would have a long haul ahead of her. Kelly looked back at Sadie. "I'm not just saying it." She patted Sadie's shoulder. "If you need someone to talk to, I'd love for you to give me a call."

Cam loved his sister. Despite all that was going on in her life, she remained a sweet, sensitive soul. Pride for her flooded him. She would be a good friend for Sadie, and Cam feared Sadie would desperately need one.

Kelly bent down in front of Ellie. "Hey, we're heading over to the movie theater to watch the new cartoon movie. Remember, the one you told me about? Would you like to go with us?"

Ellie raced over to Cam and squeezed his arm with both hands. "Daddy, can I go? Please, please, please."

"I don't see why not." He looked at Sadie. "Do you mind?" She shook her head.

Kelly grabbed Ellie's hand. "All right then. I'll take you home after the movie." She turned toward Sadie again. "I've wanted to see the comedy that just came out Friday."

"Me, too." Sadie pressed her hand to her chest. "It looks like it will be hilarious."

"Mom, we're going to be late." Kelly's youngest pulled at her sleeve.

"Okay. I'll see you."

Cam watched as Kelly and the girls made their way toward the mall's theater. Sadie's expression dropped the moment they left, and Cam knew she worried about the start of school. An idea formed in his mind. "I've been wanting to see that comedy. Why don't you and I go?"

"Now?"

"Sure. Our movie will be over about the same time as theirs. It'll save Kelly a drive to my house."

Cam could tell she mulled over the idea as she bit the inside of her lip. Finally, she grinned. "Sounds like fun."

"Great." Cam stood and picked up the shopping bags with one hand. Without thinking, he grabbed Sadie's hand. She tensed and Cam started to pull away; then she relaxed and folded her hand around his. Pleasure shot through him at her simple, soft touch. Danger horns sounded mercilessly in his mind, but he couldn't remove his hand. He knew his touch calmed her, and he hated seeing the worry behind her gaze. After all, though he fought it with all that was in him, he knew he loved her. *Knowing it doesn't mean I have to act on it.*

❧

Sadie hadn't felt this nervous since the day she'd told Ellie she was her biological mother. *That went fine. I just need to trust God that my first day of school will also go well.*

She sucked in a long breath and took one last glimpse in

her full-length mirror. Her knee-length taupe skirt and bright pink blouse were professional yet fashionable. Having decided to pull her hair back in a clip and wear a bit more makeup than usual, Sadie knew she appeared older than her twenty-four years. *Between stepping in after a wonderful thirty-year veteran occupational therapist and the possibility of the whole school system knowing I gave up my baby for adoption, I'm going to need all the help I can get at looking like a professional.*

"*Stop worrying. Remember, I am greater than your heart. I know everything.*"

Sadie released a long breath. God did know everything. He knew her exaggerated fears and worries. He knew how others would respond to her. The church members had been kind, and she knew the children she taught at church would be students in the various schools. Besides, she belonged to God. He would show her how to get through whatever lay ahead.

The story of Ruth flooded her thoughts again. How many times since deciding to move to Delaware had Sadie read the woman's story in the Old Testament? Too many times to count. Even at this moment, Sadie could hear Ruth telling Naomi that she would follow her mother-in-law anywhere, that Ruth would worship Naomi's God. *God, I know the situation is different, but I feel like Ruth. . . . I will go wherever You send me.*

Since Ellie's conception, God had shown Himself consistently faithful. He'd been there for her before that as well, when she was a girl and a teen, in good times and bad. Sadie simply hadn't acknowledged and allowed His lead with such certainty as she had since her pregnancy with Ellie.

Thank You for the reminder, Lord. I can do this through Your strength. Sadie grabbed her car keys and her purse and headed out the door.

The September morning sun was bright, and yet the air was slightly nippy. Her drive was pleasant, and she listened to her favorite praise music, allowing her soul to be rejuvenated with worship. Today, she would visit each school and meet a few of the teachers and students she would be working with. She knew introductions would probably take a few days, but she wanted to be sure she showed up at each school just the same.

After arriving at the central office, she stepped out of her car. The cool breeze felt wonderful on her cheeks, sending a soothing balm through her anxious body. *No one is going to be worried about me. I simply need to do my job and all will be fine.* She walked into the building. Anxiety started to mount again, and she was thankful she'd only eaten a container of yogurt for breakfast.

"Good morning, Sadie." The secretary at the front desk greeted her with a warm smile.

"Good morning."

She stood and lifted a good-sized office plant from the desk behind her. "This is a welcoming gift from our office. We know you'll like it here."

The beating of her heart slowed, and Sadie felt her nerves calm. She took the plant. "Thanks so much. I know I will."

She walked back to her office. Making room on the corner of her desk for the plant, she scolded herself for being so worried. She placed her purse in a desk drawer then took out the first grouping of files for the students she planned to try to meet, if only to say hello, before the day ended.

"How's it going?" The superintendent stuck his head in the door.

She smiled at the older man. "So far, so good. Thanks for the plant."

"Well, we're glad to have you." He waved then walked down the hall.

Feeling more settled, Sadie sat at her desk and turned on her computer. The bottom right-hand corner showed the time. Cam would be taking Ellie into the kindergarten room about now. Sadie yearned to go with him but wasn't sure if it would be overstepping her bounds. And Cam hadn't offered.

She envisioned Ellie, long hair swept up in a ponytail, wearing her new pink shirt and blue jean shorts. *No, I bet she wanted to wear one of her new dresses today.* It hurt that Sadie had no idea what her daughter was wearing for her first day of school. She didn't foresee Ellie crying and wanting Cam to stay with her, but one never knew what a five-year-old would do on her first day. *I want to see Ellie in the mornings. At lunch, I'll simply call Cam's cell phone and ask him. I won't know if I don't ask.*

Sadie finished the work she needed to do on the computer then grabbed her files and headed to the first elementary school. She was able to meet each of the students and teachers on her list before heading to the high school. Making her way up the stairs, she found Kelly's room—the last one on the right. She peeked in the door's window. Kelly saw her and made her way to the door.

"How's your first day going?" Kelly smiled.

"It's been great. My jittery nerves are all but gone."

"That's wonderful." Kelly's smile deepened, and Sadie noted the slight element of surprise in Kelly's tone. "Remember, if you need anything, give me a call."

"Of course." Sadie waved and walked toward the stairs. She hadn't exaggerated. Everyone had been friendly and helpful, and as lunch approached, Sadie felt more confident and comfortable about her new job. *I was just being overly sensitive this morning.*

She made her way out of the school and to her car. Once she arrived at the fast-food drive-through, Sadie flipped open her cell phone and called Cam. He answered on the first ring. "Are you busy?" Sadie asked.

"I'm working on an armoire, but I can take a quick break. How's your first day going?"

"Really well." Sadie heard the relief that sounded in her own voice.

"I'm so glad." She could tell his words were genuine, and she remembered the feel of his strong hand in hers when they walked to the movie.

"I was wondering, though, if I could come over in the mornings and maybe fix Ellie's hair before school. I really missed her this morning." *And I've missed you, too.* Sadie couldn't add that—though everything in her wanted to. She couldn't stop thinking about him.

"That sounds like a great idea. She'd love it."

Sadie got off the phone, paid and picked up her food, then drove toward Ellie's school. *The day is going much better than I ever would have anticipated, Lord. Ellie's school is next on my list. I'll have to sneak a peek into her room.*

Sadie swallowed her food before turning into the school's parking lot. After parking her car, she reapplied her lipstick and slipped a mint into her mouth.

She walked into the school and introduced herself to the secretary. The woman told her in which rooms she'd find the students she'd be working with, and Sadie made her way down the halls. Again, the teachers and students were friendly, and Sadie had already fallen in love with her job.

Trying to be discreet, Sadie peeked through the door of Ellie's classroom. The teacher sat on the carpet with a book in her hand. The students sat all around her. Miss Montgomery's expressions changed vividly as she read the book. Sadie could only see the back of Ellie's head, but by her nodding, Sadie knew Ellie was enthralled. As Sadie had guessed, her hair was in a ponytail and she wore one of her new dresses.

"May I help you?"

Sadie jumped and turned at the woman's voice. "I was just taking a peek in the room." Sadie smiled and offered her hand. "I'm Sadie Ellis, the new occupational therapist."

The woman's features softened as she took Sadie's hand. "Oh, it's nice to meet you. I'm one of the kindergarten teachers, Mrs. Black." She tapped her finger with her lip. "It seems I've heard something about you. Good, I'm sure."

Sadie's heart jumped. Why would she have heard anything about Sadie? Unless it was about Ellie. *I don't need to jump to conclusions. I may have a student in her class.*

"Well, it was nice to meet you." Sadie waved as she made her way down the hall. She stopped by the restroom then made her way back to the office.

"Yep, she's the one," Sadie heard a woman's voice say before she turned a corner. "Can you imagine giving your baby up for adoption?"

Sadie stopped. She knew they were talking about her.

"And then trying to be in the kid's life later. Sounds crazy to me," another woman responded. If Sadie was right, it sounded like Mrs. Black.

"I'll tell you, I couldn't do it," the first woman replied.

Tears welled in Sadie's eyes. She'd been foolish to think people wouldn't talk about her. Deciding to skip saying good-bye in the office, Sadie made her way back to her car. It took every ounce of composure she had to keep from bursting into tears before she made it out of the parking lot. *I'm such a fool.*

"I still know everything, Sadie, and I'm here for you."

"Oh God." Sadie swiped the tears that began to cascade down her cheeks. "I do need You. I felt such peace about coming here. I love Ellie. I love her so much. Was I wrong?"

Doesn't scripture say, "In this world you will have trouble"?

"But You, God, have overcome the world." She sniffed as she summarized the rest of the verse. "Thank You for the reminder, Lord. It has been a good day. Help me keep my mind on You and not worry about what others say."

Sadie wiped the mascara smears from beneath her eyes before she headed into her office. She let out a long breath as she sat at her desk. Checking the clock, she knew the schools had already dismissed and her day would be over in a matter of thirty minutes. Trying not to think about the women at Ellie's school, Sadie organized her files and planned her schedule for the following day.

"Knock. Knock." A familiar voice sounded just outside her door. Sadie gazed up into the kind eyes of Cam's sister, Kelly. She folded her arms in front of her chest and leaned against Sadie's door frame. "You've made it through your first day. I just thought I'd stop by and check on you before I head out to get the girls."

An unexpected wave of raw emotion overwhelmed Sadie, and tears streamed down her cheeks. Kelly stepped inside and closed the door. She pulled several tissues out of her purse and handed them to Sadie. "So the day didn't go so well?" Kelly sat in the chair in front of Sadie's desk.

Sadie shook her head. "Actually, overall the day was wonderful. Almost everyone was extremely kind and helpful."

"Almost?" Kelly's eyebrows lifted in question.

Sadie blew out a long breath. "Yeah. Almost." She wiped her nose with a tissue. "I overheard a couple of ladies at Ellie's school talking about me, and about how they couldn't believe

I would try to be in Ellie's life after I gave her up." Sadie's voice cracked, and she wiped her eyes again. "I never should have said anything to Ellie's teacher. Cam told me not to say—"

Kelly touched Sadie's hand. "Amanda Montgomery is a wonderful Christian woman. I doubt the ugliness came from her."

Sadie felt consumed with embarrassment. She'd known many a wonderful Christian to show less-than-Christlike behavior. "How do you know? What if she takes my sin out on Ellie?"

Kelly shook her head. "No. I don't think so. Besides, you can stop by her room anytime and check to see how things are going."

Sadie took a deep breath, pondering Kelly's words and remembering the Spirit's nudging. "You're right." She wiped her eyes one last time. "You know, God overcame the world. He can take care of this."

Kelly stood and wrapped her arms around Sadie's shoulders. "You're absolutely right. If God can see Cam and I both through the deaths of our spouses, he will take care of Ellie's kindergarten year. . .and your first year here."

Sadie felt humbled by the comparison of loss that Kelly and her brother had experienced to the momentary embarrassment Sadie faced. She had no right to feel as she did. "You're right, Kelly." She pulled away from Kelly's embrace. "So how was your day? What can I do to help you?"

twelve

Cam opened and closed his fist. His hand still ached from holding Sadie's hand several days before at the mall. Everything he touched reminded him, either by comparison or by contrast, of the softness of her skin. *This is nuts.* He tossed Ellie's sundress into the washing machine. *I was married for years, and here I'm acting like a lovesick middle school boy over that woman.* He growled as he poured laundry detergent over the load of clothes.

He glanced at the clock. It was still early, but he assumed Sadie would show up at any time to get Ellie ready for school. *Why did I agree to this? The woman already haunts me at night. Now, after a good whiff of her in the morning, I'll think about her all day, too.*

He scratched at his jaw. He hadn't showered or shaved this morning. His old basketball shorts that he wore to bed still hung from his waist. He picked at one of the many holes splattering his T-shirt. *I should have gotten ready before now. Having her come over here has messed up my whole morning.*

Cam made his way to Ellie's room. She lay curled in a ball under her covers, holding her blanket over her cheek. He pushed a tendril of hair away from her face. She looked like an angel, so much like her mother. A vision of Sadie sleeping filtered into his mind, and he shook the thought away. Cam gently tugged at the covers. "Wake up, pun'kin."

"Humph." Ellie grunted and gripped the comforter tighter.

The doorbell rang, and Cam took a deep breath as he made his way to the front of the house. *Lord, help me through this.* He opened the door and inwardly growled. Sadie looked adorable in a green shirt and polka-dotted skirt. She wore a matching headband in her hair and a few small pieces of gold jewelry. The whole getup made the green in her eyes shine, and if he was right, it appeared she had some gorgeous flecks of gold complementing that green. Her lips glistened with some kind of pink gloss, and it took every ounce of strength within him not to press those lips against his. In her hand was her infamous oversized cup of French vanilla, extra-cream java. Holding his snarl at bay, Cam opened the door wide. "Come on in."

"Is she up yet?" Her voice carried a higher lilt than usual, and Cam knew she hoped to be the one to wake Ellie.

"Nope."

"Great." Sadie whisked past him. The smell of her coffee mingled with the light scent of her perfume. Even her scent drove him to insanity.

Cam shut the door and padded his way to his bedroom. As it turned out, he was glad he hadn't gotten ready for work. It would give him something to do besides watching Sadie's every move while she got Ellie ready for school. "If you don't mind, I'll dress for work while you get Ellie ready."

"Sounds good," Sadie called from Ellie's room.

Cam could hear muffled sounds of laughter from his daughter before he started the shower. He turned the temperature a bit cooler than he normally liked. *Anything to keep my mind off that woman.*

It didn't take Cam much time to shower, shave, and dress. Within moments, he walked back into the kitchen. Ellie sat at the table with a bowl of cereal in front of her. Sadie stood behind Ellie's chair, once again tying her hair in long knots. French braids, Sadie had told him they were called.

"Hi, Daddy."

"Good morning, pun'kin." Cam patted her nose with his index finger.

"Mommy picked out my dress." She turned in her chair to show him what she was wearing.

"Hold still, Ellie, or I'll have to start over." Sadie's voice was kind but firm. Her maternal instincts were strong, and Cam couldn't deny what a terrific mother she'd already proven to be.

"Okay, Mommy."

"So where's my breakfast?" Cam teased.

Sadie blushed and shrugged her shoulders. "I didn't know what you liked, but I left the cereal on the counter."

"I'm just teasing you." Cam walked over to the counter and poured cereal into a bowl. Her blushes were entirely too cute. He needed to avoid unnecessary interaction with Sadie.

"All done." Sadie's voice filled the room. "You look awfully pretty."

"I'm going to go see." Ellie jumped out of her chair and raced to the bathroom.

Sadie grabbed her coffee off the table and took a drink. She looked at Cam. "She is so much fun."

"Humph." Cam took a bite of his cereal. "She's not usually this happy in the morning."

Sadie lifted one eyebrow and cocked her head. "Maybe someone else is a bit of a grouch in the morning."

Her tone and gaze were teasing and entirely too tempting. Cam looked away. "I don't know about that."

"Well, it seems to me. . ."

Blocking out the sweetness of her voice, Cam took a long swig of his coffee, strong and black, with none of the fanciness of Sadie's.

"I'm ready, Daddy." Ellie stood before him, already wearing her backpack.

Cam smiled at his daughter. *Saved by the kid.* The attraction he felt for Sadie was ridiculous, but he could not succumb to it. Even if she were attracted to him, he would never be able to give her all she wanted. *She deserves more.*

"Let me get your lunch out of the refrigerator." Cam grabbed her lunch box then turned toward Ellie.

Sadie bent down and gave his daughter a hug. She tickled Ellie's chin. "You have a good day."

Ellie giggled, and Sadie stood then wiped the wrinkles from her skirt. She pushed her hair back behind her shoulder. "I wanted to ask you something, Cam."

"Okay." Cam swallowed the knot in his throat. The look in Sadie's eyes was serious. He watched as she started to wring her hands together.

"I was wondering. . ." She shifted her weight from one foot to the other. "If you might want to get together. . ." She shrugged her shoulders. "For lunch, maybe."

"To talk about Ellie?"

"Or maybe just talk."

Cam's heart sank. Everything in him wanted to get together for lunch. He wanted to talk about her, what she yearned for in life, what her passions were. He'd gathered several of her heart's desires from the time they'd spent together with Ellie, but he couldn't deny he wanted his own time with her.

But he couldn't. He wouldn't do that to her. "I don't think so."

Sadie's gaze moved to the floor. He saw pink race up her neck and into her cheeks. "Okay. I just thought since we had a good time at the movies. . ." She brushed her hand across her cheek, probably trying to push hair that wasn't there from her eyes. A habit, he presumed. "I'd better be going. Bye, Ellie." She bent down for one last hug then swept out the door.

I am such a fool. She has no idea how much I want to spend time with her. I just can't.

Why don't you tell her why?

Heat washed over his body. The reason was humiliating. It had taken him years to feel like a full man after he'd learned the truth. He still struggled with it at times. No, the last thing he wanted to do was tell her the truth.

&

Oh dear God, I'm so humiliated. Sadie looked in her rearview mirror for the thousandth time. Though she'd driven all the way to work, her cheeks still shone bright pink after the conversation with Cam. She leaned back against the headrest. "Why did I ask him that? Girls are supposed to let the guys ask them out."

I wasn't really asking him out, she argued with herself. *I just thought we'd go to lunch and maybe see what happens.*

She looked at her reflection again and tried to convince herself aloud. "After all, he held my hand as we walked to the movie. Isn't that kind of dropping hints at a girl? Guys don't just hold hands with friends, do they?"

Shaking her head, she grabbed her purse out of the passenger's seat and opened the door. "This is ridiculous. I can't believe I'm arguing with myself over this."

She greeted the secretary with a forced smile and walked back to her office. After turning on her computer, she sifted through several files on her desk. *I will not think about him. It's my first week of school and I still have students to meet.* She transferred the files to her shoulder bag then pulled her lip gloss and compact from her purse. After applying the light pink shade, she smacked her lips together and scooped up her purse and bag. "First stop is the middle school."

The middle school had been built on a hill just several

hundred yards away from the central office. If it hadn't been Sadie's first week, she would have simply hiked the hill and enjoyed the fresh air and exercise. Not wanting to walk in with disheveled hair and clothes and inhaling deep breaths from the foot excursion, she'd opted to go ahead and drive her car. *Once I feel more settled, I'll enjoy the walk.* She pursed her lips. *Today I could use a good brisk walk.*

She huffed at the memory of Cam's rejection as she waited for the middle school secretary to electronically unlock the door to allow her inside. So much more security was needed since she'd been in middle school herself, just over a decade before. When the door clicked, Sadie plastered a smile on her lips, praying that it at least appeared genuine. She extended her hand to the secretary. "Hello. I'm Sadie Ellis, the new occupational therapist."

Before the woman had a chance to respond, a familiar voice sounded from the hall behind her office space. "Well, hello, Sadie." Charles Mann appeared, his smile as bright as she remembered. "This is Evelyn." He pointed to the secretary, and she nodded. "Come on back and I'll introduce you to a few more people."

Sadie felt herself relax at Charles's genuine welcome. "Okay." She looked at Evelyn. "It was nice to meet you."

The woman nodded, and Sadie followed Charles through several rooms attached to the back of the office. As he introduced her to people, Sadie repeated their names several times in her mind, hoping to remember them on a future day.

"Here's my office." He gestured toward a door. "Come on in and we'll talk a minute."

Sadie smiled. It was nice that he wanted to talk to her. His interest soothed her pride a bit after Cam's cool rejection that morning. Walking inside, she took in the historical decor filling his office. "You must have been a social studies teacher before you were a principal."

"How'd you guess?" His gaze swept through his office. "I especially love Revolutionary War memorabilia. Delaware has a lot of interesting places where I can find more information." He cocked his head. "Maybe I can take you with me sometime."

Sadie's pulse raced. She wasn't really interested in Charles in that way. He seemed like a great guy—nice looking, kind personality, and he obviously liked kids or he wouldn't be a principal. *Why shouldn't I be interested in him?* She contemplated the thought, knowing her lack of interest stemmed from how she felt about Cam. *Well, I might as well forget that.* She stood straighter and lifted her chin. "That might be fun."

Charles's eyebrows rose. "So how is school going so far?"

"Good." She patted her bag. "I'm here to meet a few of my students."

Charles nodded. He studied her for several moments, and Sadie could tell he mulled something over in his mind. He leaned against his desk before he spoke. "I guess you had reason to go to kindergarten orientation after all."

So the gossip has even spread to the middle school. Ah, well, soon enough something more interesting will come along to talk about. Sadie pushed her bag higher on her shoulder. She had no idea where this was going. Really, he had no right to question her past. "Yeah, I did."

Charles smiled, and his gaze softened. "The rumor mill, you know. I'm sure you know all about that."

Ha. Boy, did she ever. News spread fast when she'd gotten pregnant and then was dumped by her boyfriend. Not everyone at her college church had been thrilled with the idea of helping out the "sinner." Many believed she'd made her bed and should now lie in it.

It shouldn't surprise her that people were quick to judge, and yet that was one of the blessings God had given her during that difficult time. She'd been judged and humbled to the place that she always wanted to lend mercy to those who'd messed up. Even now, hard as it was, she knew those who spoke ill of her had hurts of their own they were avoiding.

"Yes, I know."

"Not everyone thinks badly."

Sadie studied Charles's expression. The kindness mixed with concern on his face filled her with gratitude and reminded her that he was right. The truth was just the truth. Some people yearned to dwell on the bad. Others focused on how God had redeemed. In that moment, Sadie knew Charles tended to take the latter view, and her respect for him grew. "You're right about that."

"I wonder." Charles folded his arms in front of his chest. "Is your little girl as pretty as you?"

Sadie laughed. "She definitely looks like me."

"Then she's definitely beautiful." Charles unfolded his arms and gripped the side of his desk. "I was wondering if you might be free for dinner on Friday."

Sadie debated her response. Her feelings for Cam couldn't just be turned off in a moment, and she didn't want to lead Charles on. And yet she might have considered Charles a great catch if she'd never met Cam. *Quit overanalyzing. It's just one date.* Sadie smiled. "I would love to."

"Great. I'll pick you up at six."

"Six it is." Light on her feet, Sadie glided out of the office. *A date will be fun.* Her mind whirled with thoughts of what to wear, then shifted to Ellie and Cam. With each step she took, her legs grew heavier. It just didn't feel right.

thirteen

Sadie gazed out the passenger's window of Charles's car. Though fall would be upon them in less than a month's time, the sun bathed the rolling hills in glorious beauty. Various shades of green painted the ground and trees and were accented by a splattering of white, pink, and purple wildflowers. Despite the air-conditioned car, Sadie could feel the warmth of the day outside. As they passed a pond set in a valley of sorts and surrounded by trees, she longed for Charles to stop the car and allow her to slip off her shoes and dip her feet in the water.

The week had passed faster than Sadie could have imagined. She'd been in a whirlwind at work, meeting students and colleagues, updating files, taking notes. She'd gone home late and exhausted each night. Outside of getting ready for school in the morning and attending church on Wednesday night, Sadie'd had only a few phone conversations with Ellie. She'd had virtually no contact with Cam. It surprised her how much she missed him.

I've got to stop thinking about Cam. He made it clear he's not interested. She glanced at Charles and forced herself to grin. *Besides, I'm on a date with another guy.*

"You like pizza?" Charles's voice was smooth and light.

"Love it." *Yes, let's talk. I need to keep my mind off the brown-haired, hazel-eyed, never-ending five o'clock shadow on his firm, square jaw. . . . Ugh! I've got to stop it.*

"Great." Charles's voice interrupted her wayward thoughts. "I'm taking you to one of my favorite restaurants."

Sadie studied Charles's profile. She'd figured him to be a guy who would want to fine-dine her, impress her with his eloquence. She took in his casual outfit of a red polo and jeans then glanced down at the soft yellow material of her sundress. A small, delicate floral pattern trimmed the neck, straps, and waist, making her look and feel very feminine; but it was definitely one of her fancier sundresses. *I think I've misjudged him a bit. He seems to be more of a down-to-earth kind of guy. More like Cam.*

She balled her fists and crossed her arms in front of her chest. *Sadie Ellis, you are not thinking about Cam Reynolds any more today.*

"So tell me about yourself." Charles's voice saved her from reprimanding herself further.

Sadie shrugged. "There's really not much to tell. You know where I work. You know I have a daughter. What would you like to know?"

"Do you go to church?"

"Yes. I've been attending with my daughter."

"So you're a Christian?"

Sadie looked at Charles. He gazed back at her, his expression hopeful. "Yes."

"I knew it. That's great." Charles smacked the top of the steering wheel. He looked at the road then peeked back at Sadie. He let out a loud laugh. "Don't be offended by my asking. I found myself in a relationship several years ago with a gal who didn't share my faith. It ended poorly. I like to be sure on a first date now."

Sadie furrowed her eyebrows. She studied Charles's face. His sincerity and openness were intriguing. "I understand perfectly. I'm glad you asked."

Sadie looked out the windshield. The trees and grass grew

sparse as they neared Wilmington, the "corporate capital of America," as the city was known. She preferred the quiet country setting of their town but couldn't deny her growing excitement at what Charles had planned. "So tell me about this pizza. What kind do you like?"

"My favorite is plain ol' pepperoni, thick crust, smothered in cheese. I tell them to pile it on." Charles licked his lips dramatically. "Mmm-mmm. A large Coke on the side. It's got to be a dish we'll eat in heaven."

Sadie chuckled at his enthusiasm. "It sounds fattening."

Charles put his hand around Sadie's wrist, connecting his thumb to his middle finger. "You're a scrawny little thing. A little fattening won't hurt you."

Sadie laughed. "Did you just call me scrawny?"

"Oh, come on, now. You're a beanpole. A skinny-mini as my sister would say. A regular Olive Oyl from those old Popeye cartoons."

Sadie howled. Charles certainly did not fit the hole in which she had pegged him. He was a character—a guy who could take her mind off her troubles. The big brother she'd never had. "Oh, I'll show you Olive Oyl. I'll eat you under the table."

He parked the car and swiped the keys out of the ignition. "Bring it on."

Before he had time to open her door, Sadie jumped out of the car. She hefted her purse higher on her shoulder and practically raced him to the front door of the restaurant. The Italian aroma permeated the air, even outside, and Sadie pressed her stomach to keep it from growling. She was starving, so Charles was in trouble. She'd make herself sick before she'd allow him to eat more food than her.

Charles opened the door for her. The room was huge, the walls painted a coffee brown. Italian cartoon chefs and cooking utensils adorned the walls. Red vinyl booths and chairs filled the room. A jukebox, playing old rock-and-roll music, sat against the far wall. "What a fun place."

"I told you it was great." Charles addressed the hostess. "Table for two."

The woman nodded and picked up two menus. "Right this way."

Sadie continued to gaze around the room as she followed Charles and the hostess. The atmosphere was endearing, and the smells tantalizing. She wondered what other music the jukebox contained. There were a few oldies she would love to hear.

Her chest tightened when she spied a small girl sitting with her back to Sadie at a table across the room. The lighting was dim, but Sadie could tell the child had long brown hair, swept into a ponytail. She appeared to be Ellie's age. *That would be impossible. I mean, what are the chances?*

Sadie looked at the person who sat across from the girl. Her gaze locked with the eyes of that person. *It can't be.*

❧

Cam sat stone still. *It can't be.* He blinked several times to clear his vision, and yet there she still stood in front of a booth across the room from him.

With another man.

Fury he hadn't known in years shot through him. His heart raced, and he clenched his fists. He took several deep breaths. Sadie was attracted to him—Cam— not this other guy. He knew she was. She was the mother of his daughter. She belonged to him.

Cam closed his eyes. *What am I? Some kind of Neanderthal?*

"Look, Daddy." Ellie held up the child's menu coloring page. "I colored in the lines."

Cam looked at the purple smiling Italian man holding the green pizza. "Good job."

Ellie wrinkled her nose. "Yeah, but the colors are all wrong." She held up the two crayons in her hand. "They only gave me purple and green. Do you think Mommy will like it anyway?"

Cam nodded, realizing he had to do everything in his power to keep Ellie from seeing Sadie. *Wouldn't that be great?* "I'm sure she'll love it."

Cam looked back toward the kitchen area then glanced at his watch. It had been fifteen minutes since they'd placed their order. Surely, their pizza would arrive soon. He tapped his fingertips against the table and scanned the room, trying to avoid Sadie and her date's booth. *Of course they'd be sitting directly in my line of vision.*

He couldn't help but peek at them. The man was a good-looking guy, Cam presumed. Brown hair. Average height. Closer to Sadie's age. Really white teeth. They nearly blinded Cam when the guy smiled at the waitress as he placed the order.

Cam looked at Sadie. Their gazes met again; then she looked away. She shifted in her seat, and Cam knew she was uncomfortable with him and Ellie being there. *Good. Let her squirm. She doesn't need to be dating anyway. She's a mother, after all.*

Cam growled at himself. He had no right to think like that. Sadie had invited him to lunch, and he'd turned her down. In his gut, he knew it was him, not her, who kept a possible relationship at bay. *Why does it have to be this way?*

Like you said, it's your choice. You could tell her the truth.

Cam pounded the top of the table with his fist. "It's not that easy."

"I know it, Daddy." Ellie pointed to her picture. "See, I got out of the lines right here on his hat. It's hard to stay in the lines."

Thankful she was oblivious to his inner turmoil, Cam allowed himself to chuckle at his daughter. He tweaked her nose with his thumb and finger. "You're doing a great job." She giggled, and Cam noticed that Sadie looked over at them.

"Here ya go." The server arrived with their pizza, saving him from further agony caused by thoughts of Sadie.

"Thank you," Ellie chimed to the woman then shifted in her seat until she sat on her knees. "Can I get my piece?"

"Be careful. It's hot."

"I will." Ellie struggled with the spatula and the dripping cheese until she finally maneuvered a piece onto her plate. She blew on it several times then touched it with the tip of her finger before taking a small bite. "Mmm. This is good, Daddy."

Cam placed a piece on his plate, focusing his attention on his daughter and the food. He tried to listen to Ellie's chatter, tried to think only of filling his stomach. The pizza was usually his favorite. Tonight, it had no taste. Cam sighed a breath of relief when Ellie took a last bite, leaned back in her chair, and put her hand over her tummy—her way of telling him she was stuffed. He assumed she would be unstuffed by the time they passed the nearest ice cream shop. That was fine with him. They'd made it through the entire dinner and Ellie hadn't seen Sadie. The quicker they got out of there, the better.

He peeked at her booth. The man said something then threw back his head in laughter. Sadie laughed as well then patted the side of her mouth with a napkin. Cam snarled. The scene made his stomach churn.

"Can I play something on the jukebox now, Daddy?"

"No—" Cam reached for Ellie's arm as she turned around to face the jukebox, but he was too late.

"Mommy!" Ellie's squeal ripped through the room. Cam

groaned as his child jumped out of her seat and raced to the other side of the restaurant.

"Hi, Ellie."

Cam watched, stuck to his seat, as Sadie slipped out of the booth and wrapped her arms around his daughter. *I wonder if I can get away with staying here.*

"Daddy, look—it's Mommy." She patted Sadie's shoulder then motioned for Cam to come join her. "Come here."

"Just a minute." Cam pulled his wallet out of his pocket and laid the money for their dinner and the tip on the table. Slowly, he stood and made his way over to the booth.

"So you must be Ellie," the man said. "You are every bit as beautiful as your mother."

Cam scowled.

Sadie looked up at Cam, her expression as haunted as he felt. "Cam and Ellie, this is Charles Mann. Charles, this is Cam and Ellie."

"It's a pleasure to meet you." Charles didn't seem to detect the tension as he extended his hand, a blinding smile splitting his lips.

"Sure." Cam shook the man's hand. He knew his mother would be appalled to see his lack of manners. He should be nicer, but he couldn't. The man was on a date with the woman he loved, and there was nothing he could do about it.

Tell the truth. See what happens.

He shoved the idea out of his mind. Their relationship was doomed to failure. She was the birth mother of his adopted daughter. She was ten years his junior. The attraction was ludicrous. His teen years had long passed him by, and it was time he remembered that. He didn't need a replacement for Brenda. As if anyone could replace her. Sadie was already taking on the maternal role in Ellie's life. He didn't have to be included in that. It wasn't like there weren't tons of kids out there whose mom and dad didn't live together.

But you want her in your life. "He who finds a wife finds what is good and receives favor from the Lord."

Cam gritted his teeth against his spirit. He grabbed Ellie's hand in his. "You two have fun. We'd better be going."

"But, Daddy, I want to stay with Mommy. Can't we stay just a little longer?"

"No, Ellie." Cam nodded to Charles then forced himself to smile at Sadie. The hurt in her eyes pulled at his heart. How could she be hurt? She was the one ripping his heart from his chest.

"But, Daddy. . ."

"No." He gripped her hand tighter and guided them toward the door.

"Why not?"

"Because Mommy's on a date."

"What's a date?"

Cam sighed. "It's when a boy and girl who like each other go out to dinner and maybe to a movie."

"You and Mommy should go on a date. You like each other."

From the mouths of babes. "Honey, I just don't think that's possible."

"Why?"

Because I'm a stubborn, overgrown mule. He shook his head. It wasn't because he was stubborn. He just couldn't face the look on her face, the look that Brenda'd had, the look that he would never be able to erase from his mind if he told her the truth.

fourteen

"You and Mommy should go on a date." Ellie's words echoed in Sadie's mind. She took another small bite of pizza. The cheese nearly gagged her. Or maybe it wasn't the cheese. Maybe it was the fact that seeing Cam had tied her insides into so many knots that her stomach didn't have room for anything more.

She looked at Charles. He'd quieted substantially since Cam and Ellie left. She watched as he swallowed a bite of pizza then took a drink of his Coke. He seemed to be avoiding eye contact with her. He wiped his mouth then cleared his throat. "So what movie would you like to see?"

Sadie twisted the napkin in her hand. "Charles, I don't think I can do this."

"Yeah. I didn't think so." Charles pushed his plate away and leaned back in the booth. "So you like this guy."

It wasn't a question. It was more a statement of fact, and Sadie pursed her lips. It seemed highly inappropriate to discuss her feelings for a guy when she was on a first date with another man.

Charles leaned forward, resting his elbows on the table. "It's okay. You can tell me. I admit I asked you out because I'm interested, but it's not like we've dated forever. We can be friends."

Sadie smiled at Charles. He would make a great friend. Hadn't she already thought of him as the brother she'd never had? And with so much happening in such a short time, Sadie had to admit she could use an extra friend or two. She smacked her hands onto the table in surrender. "I'm crazy about him." She shook her head. "It's totally nuts. The guy is my daughter's father, for crying out loud." She twisted in her seat. "Every time I think that, it seems preposterous, but saying it out loud. . ." She threw her hands up in exasperation.

Charles laughed. "I've got a hunch the feeling's mutual."

Sadie shook her head. "No. He's made it clear he's not interested."

"Hmm. I find that hard to believe."

"Seriously." Sadie picked at the crust of her pizza. "I wanted to go out to lunch with him, and he turned me down flat."

Charles scratched the side of his head. "I bet there's more to it than that. Have you told him how you feel?"

"Not in words, but. . ."

"Then you gotta tell him in words." Charles motioned for the waitress. "I'll take you home so you can pray about this."

"But our movie?"

"I can take you to the movie." He gazed into her eyes. "If that's what you want."

Sadie sighed. She felt physically ill from seeing Cam, and a drummer was beginning a light tapping in her head. "No. You're right. I think I'll call it a night."

Charles paid the bill then led her to his car. Sadie slipped inside and leaned against the headrest as the drummer's rhythm grew louder and more consistent. Wishing she'd brought aspirin with her, Sadie was thankful Charles didn't talk as he drove her home. Before she knew it, the car stopped.

"You're home." Charles's voice was soft.

Sadie opened her eyes and forced herself to sit up. Guilt mingled with the incessant pounding in her head. "Thanks, Charles. I'm sorry this date didn't exactly go—"

Charles lifted his hand. "Hey, it's okay. I've always been

the girl's-best-friend kind of guy." Sadie noted a twinge of frustration in his voice. He winked. "I'll be praying for you."

"Thanks." Sadie slipped out of the car, walked to her front door, and went inside. She could hear him driving off as she shut the door. She kicked off her sandals and padded to the kitchen. After finding the pain reliever, she grabbed a bottle of water from the refrigerator and took the medicine.

She made her way into her bedroom, took off her dress, and put on a pair of pajama pants and matching T-shirt. The drumming had escalated from pounding to a roar. Her stomach knotted, and she knew her chances of revisiting the pizza she'd eaten had seriously increased. Plopping onto the bed, she covered her eyes with a pillow. "God, help my head, and calm my stomach."

Sadie closed her eyes and slowed her breathing. She was no stranger to headaches, especially those brought on by stress. She knew if she calmed herself, the medicine would kick in, and she would feel better. She sucked in a long breath. *Just breathe in and out, nice and slow.*

ॐ

Sadie woke with a start. She sat up and looked around the room, blinking repeatedly to get her eyes to focus. Her bedroom light was on and she could tell it was still dark outside. She glanced at her alarm clock. It read just after nine. She frowned and rubbed her temples with her fingertips. "What day is it?"

Her date with Charles washed through her mind. Cam's pained expression when their eyes locked planted itself in her brain. "Oh yeah." Sadie fell back onto the bed. Her first real date in Delaware had been a doozy. *After all, how many girls get to go out with a great guy they don't like only to run into the man they love? Oh yeah, with their daughter.* She groaned. Her life was a complete mess.

"God, I need some help."

"*I'm always here for you.*" Her spirit prodded her. She grinned and leaned over to pick up her Bible off the end table. Planning to open to the concordance to seek verses that might soothe her heart and thoughts, the book opened to a page with a sticky note she'd written before moving to Delaware. She read the verse aloud. " 'For God is greater than our hearts, and he knows everything.' First John 3:20."

She looked up at the ceiling. "God, You know everything. And You are greater than my heart. Take away these feelings I have for Cam."

Maybe the feelings aren't wrong. Maybe the fear is.

Sadie frowned at the thought. She knew the heart was deceitful above all things. She couldn't trust her feelings. She had to base her actions on what she *knew* was right in scripture. *Is it wrong that I love Cam? Does it go against God's Word? Or is it the fear in my heart that God is greater than?*

The thought gave Sadie pause. She brushed a strand of hair away from her face. Charles's encouragement to tell Cam how she felt flooded her mind.

"I do love him, God."

"*Tell him.*"

"But what if he rejects me?"

"*I know everything.*"

"Okay, what's the worst that could happen?" A vision of him smacking his leg bent over in raucous laughter drifted into her mind. *Okay, maybe I won't think that way.* Sadie's body trembled with excitement and trepidation. She slipped on a pair of sandals, grabbed her purse, and bolted out the door to her car.

Ellie would be in bed by now, so she would be able to talk with Cam alone. As she shifted her car into drive, she noticed she still wore her blue and white star pajamas. She smacked her forehead. "I didn't even get dressed."

With a sigh of determination, she shook her head. "It doesn't matter. If I don't do this now, I'll chicken out later."

❧

After flipping through channel after channel, Cam turned off the television. He grabbed his empty cereal bowl from the end table and made his way toward the kitchen. The last thing he wanted to watch was some reality show where a guy had to choose a potential wife from a group of beautiful women. Nor did he want to be entertained by sitcoms portraying a guy with the girl of his dreams, only to have her reject him in some cruel, inhumane way. Even the football game was showing a special report on one of the NFL's quarterbacks and how he and his wife met and married. He shoved the bowl and spoon into the dishwasher. *I need some fresh air.*

Cam made his way to Ellie's room. He stepped inside the door. As usual, Ellie was curled in a ball under her comforter, her special blanket nestled against her face. Her long eyelashes fanned her cheek in sweet, restful sleep. Leaning over, he brushed a light kiss on her forehead then tiptoed out of the room, partially closing the door behind him.

He walked out the back door and gingerly closed it behind him. If Ellie did wake up, she would be able to see him at the pond. He jammed his hands in his jeans pockets and watched his step along the short trail. How many nights had he spent sitting on the bench in front of these calm waters? The spot was his safe haven, his place to allow God to refresh his body and spirit. He looked at his bench. Someone was there.

Balling his fists, he stomped toward the stranger. No one would threaten the safety of his daughter. If this person planned to scope out a way to get into his home, the intruder would have to go through him first.

As Cam drew closer, the moonlight shone brighter on the person's form. *It's a woman.* Cam unclenched his fists. *Who in the world would be out here at this time of night? And what would she want?*

Kelly's girls were still too young to have traveled to his house alone, and the woman didn't have the same shape as Kelly. She turned her face to look at something to her left. Cam stopped as he drank in the profile.

Sadie.

Unsure what to do, Cam stood watching her for several moments. She was oblivious to his presence, and he could tell by the movement of her hands and head that she was having a conversation with herself, or maybe with God. It was late, but it wasn't *that* late. Cam wondered why she wasn't still on her date. And she wasn't wearing the same gorgeous dress she'd been wearing at the pizza place. Cam had felt a jealousy he'd never known in his life when he saw her all dressed up for another man.

What is she doing here?

Cam took a step closer. A twig snapped beneath his feet, and Sadie jumped up then turned around. She placed her hand over her chest and took several deep breaths. "Oh, Cam, you scared the life out of me."

Cam took in the blue T-shirt with a large white star on the front and the oversized blue pajama pants covered in matching smaller white stars. Her hair was tossed up into some sort of knot with strands of hair sticking out at all angles. *And this is how she gets dressed for me.* He bit back a smile at the thought. Actually, she looked amazing—like a woman he could wrap his arms around and not mess up. He scratched his jaw, already in desperate need of a shave. "Well,

I didn't exactly expect to see you out here. Aren't you supposed to be on a date?"

"I was, but Charles took me home after we ate." Sadie clasped her hands in front of her and rocked back and forth on the balls of her feet.

Cam nodded. "Okay."

Cam waited for her to say something else, but Sadie just stood there staring at the tree beside her. Cam looked at the pond, then up at the moon, and finally back at Sadie. He had no idea what she wanted and no clue what to say. He didn't want to know if her date went well, didn't want to know if she liked the guy. Quite frankly, at that moment, he didn't really care if she wanted to see or talk about Ellie. He needed time to lick his wounds, the cuts that would never be able to heal from his inability to make her his own.

"Cam, we need to talk."

Finally, she speaks. Cam raised his eyebrows and pursed his lips. If he had a dime for every time that woman had said those words—but right now, he was not interested in talking.

"Please, Cam."

He looked into her pleading eyes. He could barely see the green in the dimness of the moonlight, but he could tell they implored him to give what she asked. The woman's eyes were his nemesis, and he knew better than to look into them. He smacked his hand to his thigh. "Fine."

She lifted one side of her mouth into somewhat of a grin. "You're not going to make this easy, are you?"

Easy? What was he making or not making easy? The woman he loved walked into a pizza parlor—looking irresistibly amazing and smelling unbelievably edible—with another man. Right in front of him. She had no idea how *hard* she'd been on him.

"I know I'm ten years younger than you." Sadie clasped her hands together.

Keep scraping the wound, woman.

She stepped closer to him. She bit her bottom lip, and he could tell she was breathing heavier. "And I know Brenda was your wife, and that you loved her." She grabbed his hand, caressing his palm with her thumb. "You have to know how much I cared for Brenda."

Cam held his breath. Her hand, so soft against his, sent electricity coursing through his veins. Every fiber within him wanted to scoop her into his arms.

She reached up her free hand, tracing her fingertips across the stubble along his jaw. Allowing her gaze to penetrate his, she turned her head up slightly. "I've fallen for you, Cam. I believe I love—"

All sense of restraint washed out of his body. He cupped her cheeks in his hands and lowered his lips to hers. She welcomed the kiss, and Cam felt his head swirl with desire. He loved this woman. He wanted this woman. Knowing he couldn't act on his feelings, he pulled away. Taking deep breaths, he peered into her eyes, filled with love and passion. She touched her bottom lip, her eyes begging him for an answer. "Please tell me you feel the same way?"

He brushed an escaped tendril of hair away from her cheek. "You have no idea how I feel."

"I love you, Cam."

Guilt, remorse, truth swept through him. He dropped his hand from her cheek. "I'm sorry, Sadie."

"Why, Cam?" Sadie grabbed his hand in hers. "Why are you sorry? You do have feelings for me. I see it in your eyes. I felt it in your kiss."

Cam swallowed hard. Humiliation filled his heart. He didn't

want to tell her. He didn't want to see the look in her eyes. Couldn't stand the mixture of sadness and pity that would cover her beautiful face.

But he had to tell her. He couldn't just let her believe she meant nothing to him. "Sadie." Her gaze begged for a reason. He could see the fear of rejection in her beautiful green eyes. *I won't look at her face. Then I won't see the expression.* He pulled his hand away as he lifted his face toward the sky and stared at the moon. "I can't have children. Brenda and I adopted because of me, not her. I won't do that to another woman."

fifteen

Sadie's whole body had felt numb for two days. She'd opened up to Cam, even told him she loved him, and his response was to say he couldn't have children. He hadn't told her he loved her as well. Part of her believed he did. She touched her lips. His kiss, the look in his eyes—they spoke of true, deep affection. But what if his inability to have kids was just his way of saying he didn't want to have feelings for her?

And how do I feel about him not being able to have kids? Sure, Sadie had already been given the opportunity to carry a child in her womb, but she'd never experienced first smiles, first steps, first times to the potty. She wanted to be a mother more than she wanted to be an occupational therapist. Her deepest desire was to be a wife and mom. Could she be happy being the mother of only Ellie?

She rolled over in her bed, rubbing her temples with her fingertips. "Oh, I don't want to think about this anymore." She peered at the alarm clock beside her bed. "Well, I've definitely missed church." She forced herself to sit up. It was just as well. She didn't feel ready to see Cam again.

I'm going to have to get over it pretty soon. I'm not going to disappoint Ellie by missing getting her ready for school tomorrow morning. Forcing her legs over the side of the bed, she knew she at least needed to get ready and make her way to the store. She'd been out of laundry detergent for three days. Her clothes would be walking themselves to the washing machine if she didn't do something about them.

After showering, fixing her hair and makeup, and eating some breakfast, Sadie grabbed her Bible. She hated that she'd missed church and wanted to be sure she got some Bible study in her before leaving the house. Having just finished a women's Bible study a few days before, Sadie was unsure what to read. She didn't want to begin reading through the Bible because she already knew of another study she planned to pick up at the bookstore the following day.

She flipped through the pages. "Hmm, God. What can I read in a day?" The Psalms were always worshipful and uplifting, but she kind of felt like a story. Esther was one of her favorite books of the Bible, but she definitely wasn't in a "queen" mood. "God, I sound ridiculous. Your entire Word is breathed by You. You can speak to me in any chapter in any book. Show me, Lord."

The pages seemed to open to the book of Ruth. Perfect. Ruth had been on her heart for weeks. She started to read about Naomi and Elimelech and their two boys. She read about their move to the pagan land of Moab. By the end of chapter 1, all the men in Naomi's family had died, and she and her daughter-in-law Ruth were heading back to Naomi's homeland of Bethlehem. The story was so familiar to Sadie that she found herself speed-reading through the verses.

Then she reached chapter 3. Her reading slowed as she put herself into the character of Ruth. Naomi essentially asked Ruth to throw herself at the feet of Boaz, her kinsman-redeemer. In complete humility and vulnerability, Ruth obeyed by lying at his uncovered feet on the threshing floor. When he awoke, Ruth asked him to marry her. Actually, she said to spread the corner of his garment over her, but that was essentially a proposal from her.

Sadie thought of her admission of love to Cam two nights

before. His response had been completely different from Boaz's. Boaz raced to the town gate to claim Ruth as his bride before the day ended. Cam had rejected Sadie.

Did he really reject you?

It sure felt like a rejection. Her lips tingled as the memory of his kiss swept through her. The kiss hadn't felt like rejection at all. *God, please just show me what I'm supposed to do.*

Sadie closed her Bible and held it to her chest for a moment. She loved God's Word and knew every bit of it spoke truth. Today, she'd felt led to look at Ruth. God would show her why. She stood and slipped on her sandals. After grabbing her purse off the chair, she walked out to her car. *I'm watching for what you want to show me, Lord.*

Dark clouds hung low in the sky, and Sadie knew at any moment rain would burst forth from them. The temperature had begun to drop. It would be no time at all before she'd have to start wearing fall clothes. She could hardly believe she'd been in Delaware that long. Already Ellie was halfway through being five years old.

As Sadie pulled into the grocery store parking lot, rain began to pelt her windshield. *I guess it's time to put an umbrella in the car.* She opened the door, covered her head with her purse, and raced inside. The store's air conditioner hit her with cold air, and Sadie shivered as she selected a grocery cart. She nodded and smiled at one of the cashiers as she walked to the fruit and vegetable section. *I should have made a list,* Sadie scolded herself as she selected a few apples, dropped them in a bag, then placed them in the cart.

She meandered down the bread aisle, picking up a loaf of wheat bread and a bag of bagels. She tapped her lip with her fingertip. *What did I come for to begin with?* She snapped her fingers. *Laundry detergent.*

Sadie made her way to the detergent aisle. A blond-haired woman stood in front of the brand Sadie liked. Sadie noticed a car seat clipped to the lady's cart. Taking a quick peek at the baby, Sadie couldn't help but smile at the beautiful Asian child.

"I'm sorry." The woman maneuvered her cart so that Sadie could get by.

"You're fine." She pointed to the child. "Your baby is adorable."

"Thanks." The woman adjusted the blanket around the baby's legs. "We've only had her a couple weeks."

Sadie frowned. The child wasn't old, but it was apparent she was more than just a couple of weeks.

"We adopted her," the woman continued. "She's our second daughter from China."

Sadie's heart skipped as she smiled at the woman and her baby. "Well, she sure is beautiful."

"Thanks." The woman pushed the cart down the aisle.

Sadie grabbed a container of her favorite detergent and placed it in her cart. She chuckled to herself. How could she, of all people, not have thought of adoption? She didn't physically have to carry a baby. God provided children in various ways—birth, foster care, adoption. She loved Cam. She loved Ellie. Future children would be in God's hands.

Her chest grew heavy with excitement. She'd simply tell Cam she didn't care that he couldn't have biological children. Then he could. . .

God, he never said he cared for me. Granted, I didn't uncover his feet and lie down in front of them, but Cam surely didn't act as if he'd go running to the town gate to claim me either.

The heaviness in her heart shifted from excitement to weariness. *But I do love him, Lord. What should I do?*

❧

"Someone is a bit on the grumpy side today." Kelly picked up their dirty lunch dishes, stacking them on top of each other.

Cam pushed away from the table and stood. He grabbed a few dishes and followed Kelly into the kitchen. "Don't worry about these. I'll get them later."

Kelly swatted the air. "Hogwash. My girls and I just devoured all the lunchmeat and cheese in your fridge. The least I can do is stick these in the dishwasher."

Cam nodded. "Okay. Thanks." He snapped the lids on the mustard and mayonnaise and stuck them back in the refrigerator.

"So what gives?"

Cam looked back at his sister. In only a moment's time, she already had all the plates in the dishwasher and a few of the glasses. He shrugged. "Nothing gives."

"Humph. Don't give me that." Kelly wiped a splash of water off her cheek with her shoulder. "You forget who you're talking to. I know when something is up. I was there for your diaper changings."

Cam grunted. "Oh yeah. You were two. I'm sure Mom had you changing all my diapers."

She lifted her index fingers. "I didn't say I changed them. I said I was there."

Cam rolled his eyes. "Like I said. Nothing."

"I noticed Sadie wasn't at church this morning." She placed the last two glasses in the dishwasher then wiped her hands on a towel. Turning toward Cam, she added, "I'm surprised she's not here right now."

Cam blew out a long breath. He had known this was coming. Though he had no desire to discuss the relationship, or lack thereof, with Kelly, he knew it was inevitable. "Where are the girls?"

Kelly dropped the towel on the counter. "Outside at the pond. Fishing."

"In the afternoon?"

"My girls don't care about the best time of day to fish. They just like to do it when they can." Kelly sat down at the table then patted the chair beside her. "Now quit stalling and tell me what happened."

Cam plopped into the chair. "Well, Sadie told me she loves me."

"That's great. You love her. It's as plain as the nose on your face."

Cam raked his fingers through his hair then smacked the table. "It's not great."

"Okay, so she's a little younger than you, and I admit this is not your normal situation with her being Ellie's birth mother and all, but you said yourself that Brenda loved Sadie, that they'd corresponded through the whole pregnancy and then after Ellie was born. . . ."

Cam glared at his sister. "It's not that and you know it."

"What then, Cam?"

"She wants children." Cam spit the words through gritted teeth. He'd had to admit his shortcoming so many times in the last few days he felt physically ill over it. *God, I thought I'd given this to You, but it's beyond humiliating.*

"Did you tell her?"

"Yes."

"What did she say?"

"Nothing."

"What do you mean 'nothing'?"

Cam pushed away from the table. "I mean she didn't say

anything. She just left." Through with the conversation, Cam trudged into the living room. He stood beside the back door watching the girls at the pond.

"I think you need to talk to her some more, Cam." Kelly moved from the table. He could feel her presence just mere feet from him.

"What's there to talk about?" He turned and smacked his hand against his leg. "I won't do that to her, Kelly. You didn't see the devastation on Brenda's face when we learned we could never have our own kids." He shook his head to keep from remembering the pain in her eyes.

That stupid accident. The memory of his bike wreck when he'd been only ten years old flooded his mind. The doctor couldn't say for sure it had caused Cam's sterility, but the doctor had seen it happen before. It was the only possible cause Cam could think of that he couldn't have children.

"This is different. Sadie knows the truth beforehand. You need to talk with her. If she's told you she loves you—"

"I won't marry—"

"Whoa. Marry?" Kelly lifted her hand. "Cam, if you are considering marriage with Sadie, then you owe it to the both of you to at least discuss this." She grabbed the doorknob. "I'm going to check on the girls. You need to do some praying."

Cam scowled as he watched Kelly walk toward the pond. She didn't understand. She couldn't. Brenda's mother had a terrible time conceiving. They'd just assumed their fertility problems stemmed from her. Brenda had gone through several test and treatments, some more uncomfortable than others. Month after month, he watched her heart break when the pregnancy test came back negative. *God, I can't do that to Sadie. She's young. She could have several children.*

"This is different. Sadie knows the truth beforehand." Kelly's

words popped into his mind. It was a different situation. Sadie could make a conscious decision to love him despite everything. But he could also choose not to do that to her.

The back door opened, and Ellie walked inside. She held her stomach, her face pale as powder. "I don't feel so good, Daddy."

"Are you going to throw up?" Cam no sooner asked the question than Ellie vomited all over the floor. "Okay then." Cam scooped Ellie into his arms and raced to the bathroom. The nauseating smell burned his nostrils before he'd had the chance to hold his breath.

Ellie's little body shook as tears welled in her eyes. "I still don't feel good." Her stomach heaved just as Cam got her in front of the commode.

Cam held her hair with one hand and patted her back with the other. *Nothing like a little upchuck to keep a guy's mind off his troubles.*

sixteen

Cam looked at the clock above the kitchen table. *Two o'clock in the morning, and I feel like I'm dying.* Cam had washed four loads of laundry and scrubbed the living room floor and the bathroom floor, and now he had to scrub Ellie's mattress. The poor child had thrown up no less than six times since that afternoon. And never in the same place twice.

He sighed. The smell of detergent, bleach, and vomit made his stomach churn. Hopefully, Ellie would feel better soon. She was running only a low-grade fever, and Cam presumed she'd caught some kind of stomach bug. *Well, she did start school last week. All kinds of new germs to grow immune to.*

"Daddy." Ellie's soft whimper sounded from his room. He'd laid her in his bed, a clean bucket on the floor beside her. This time he'd wised up and put a tarp beneath the covers. If she missed the bucket, which she tended to do, and threw up in his bed, she'd only soil the blankets, not the mattress as well.

"Coming, pun'kin." Cam walked into his room. He leaned over and gently rubbed her forehead. "What is it? Do you need a little sip of water?"

Ellie shook her head. "I want Mommy."

Cam's heart clenched. "Pun'kin, Mommy's not here."

Tears formed in Ellie's eyes. "Please, Daddy. I want Mommy."

"Ellie."

The tears spilled down her pale cheeks as her little chest heaved up and down. "Mommy." Her bottom lip puckered weakly, and Cam could tell she wasn't simply demanding her way. She genuinely wanted Sadie to comfort her while she was sick. "Please, Daddy. Mommy."

Cam bent down and kissed her forehead. "Okay. I'll call her."

❧

Sadie rushed to Cam's doorstep. She'd had limited exposure to sick children, but Cam had told her that Ellie wanted her, and nothing would stop Sadie from seeing her little girl. After only one knock, Cam opened the door and Sadie flew past him toward Ellie's bedroom.

"It's okay, sweetie." She looked at the bed, void of sheets, comforter, and most important, Ellie. She turned back to Cam, who still stood by the front door. "Where is she?"

He grinned. "In my room, across the hall."

She waved her hands in front of her nose. "It smells atrocious in here. That bleach smell is so strong I want to throw up myself. Maybe you could open a window."

"Sure."

A twinge of anxiety washed over Sadie as she walked into Cam's room. She felt something akin to an unauthorized trespasser as she took in the sage green walls accented with cream Victorian curtains. A large, dark armoire sat pristinely across from the oversized sleigh bed. The comforter, a light sage and cream color dotted with small embroidered roses, spoke nothing of Cam, only Brenda.

"Mommy?" Ellie's soft voice broke through Sadie's thoughts.

She rushed to her daughter's side. Caressing Ellie's forehead and cheek with the back of her hand, Sadie whispered, "It's okay, sweetie. I'm here."

"Mommy's here." Ellie nestled her cheek between her special blanket and Sadie's hand. She closed her eyes and let out a contented sigh.

Sadie looked back at the doorway. Cam leaned against the

frame, and again anxiety swept through her. The man she loved bored through her with his gaze. *Maybe he feels I don't belong here in his and Brenda's room, too.*

"Thanks for coming, Sadie." Cam's voice was steady, but she could hear the exhaustion in his tone. She noted the bags beneath his eyes and wondered if today wasn't the first all-nighter he'd pulled. She knew she hadn't slept more than an hour or two since the other night.

"You look pretty tired, Cam." She maneuvered her body so that the blood could pump back to her hand again. "Why don't you lie down, and I'll take it from here?"

"No. You have to work in the morning. You don't need to stay long."

She shook her head. "I already called in."

His eyebrows furrowed in a straight line. "You what?"

"We have a number we can call in the night if we have to call in sick. I already called. I'll stay with Ellie tomorrow."

"But school just started last week."

"Cam, I'm her mother." Sadie stopped and bit the inside of her lip. She looked down at the sleeping girl. "I had to give her away, but now that God's given me the chance to be with her. . ." She looked back up at Cam, her gaze begging him to understand. "Please, I want to be her mother."

Cam started to say something; then he pursed his lips and nodded. "Okay then. I'm going to make a pallet on the living room floor."

Sadie watched Cam leave then turned her attention back to Ellie. The girl's hair was matted against her forehead, but Sadie was thankful she wasn't warm to the touch. Gingerly removing her hand from Ellie's grip, Sadie arranged the covers around her daughter. In what seemed only minutes, Ellie woke up feeling sick again. Sadie was ready with a bucket and washcloth and was able to keep the mess to a minimum.

Two more times, Ellie awakened sick. By five o'clock, Sadie was about to fall asleep sitting straight up. She placed her hand on Ellie's cheek. Still no fever, and it had been over an hour since she'd vomited. *Maybe I can lie down for a minute.*

Sadie contemplated slipping into bed beside Ellie, but she didn't want to risk jarring the child's stomach. She peeked in Ellie's room. Her bedsheets weren't on the bed, and Sadie didn't want to go on a search-and-find mission to discover where Cam kept them.

The silence of the house suddenly wrapped itself around her. Realization dawned that Cam slept only one room away. *I'm sure he's as gorgeous asleep as he is awake.* Despite still struggling with his rejection, Sadie tiptoed into the living room. *I'll just take a quick peek.*

She felt a slight breeze as she walked into the living room and noticed he'd opened a window just as she'd suggested. Her gaze moved to Cam. He lay on his back with his arms up and his fingers intertwined behind his head. The man looked as if he'd settled onto the floor to take in a football game on the television, not to sleep. A light blanket covered him from his chest to the bottom of his feet. His expression was peaceful, and Sadie found herself wishing she could bend down and gently kiss his lips.

The story of Ruth slipped into her mind, and she gasped. Cam stirred, and she covered her mouth with her hand. *Oh no, no, no, no. I am not going to go lying down at that man's feet.*

Sadie's heart raced, and she covered her chest with her hand. Cam looked so perfect sleeping. He was all she wanted in a husband—a Christian who loved his Lord dearly, a man who loved her daughter and took such good care of her, a true protector and provider. He even looked like the kind of guy

Sadie had always been attracted to. *He makes the checklist I made up as a young girl.* She inwardly chuckled at the lists she and her friends used to compile for potential boyfriends.

"Go and uncover his feet and lie down." Naomi's words to Ruth filtered through her mind. Sadie shook her head. There was no way on the planet she would do what Ruth had done. Rustling blankets was no longer a sign of endearment, and it most definitely didn't stand for a wedding proposal in their day and time. *Like I'd propose to him anyway.*

The idea was ludicrous. Besides, there was no town gate for Cam to go running off to so that he could claim her as his own. She hadn't married another man—a relative of his, no less—and she didn't need a kinsman-redeemer. *The connection I feel with Ruth is crazy.*

She crossed her arms in front of her chest. Cam probably wouldn't even know what she was doing. What were the chances he was well versed on the book of Ruth? *And besides, I do have my pride.*

"Pride goes before destruction."

Sadie uncrossed her arms and raked her hand through her hair. She took several deep breaths then let her hands fall at her sides. *What have I got to lose? I love the man. God, I believe You brought me to Delaware for more reasons than I'd ever originally imagined. I'm going to trust You to help me through the humiliation if Cam laughs in my face.*

❧

Something jolted Cam awake. He blinked his eyes then wiped them with the back of his hands. Looking at his watch, he noted it was only six in the morning. A slight breeze blew through the window, and Cam curled his toes at its coolness. *No wonder. I pulled the covers off my feet.*

Cam sat up and grabbed the bottom of the blanket. *What*

in the world? Sadie was lying at his feet. Her eyes were closed and her breathing seemed even. One of his throw cushions was wadded underneath her cheek. He scoffed at her sleeping on the floor without even so much as a blanket beneath her. *Why wouldn't she at least sleep on the couch? It's too small for me, but she would have fit.*

Cam jerked off his blanket with the intention of lifting her onto the couch when he saw his Bible sitting above Sadie's head. *I keep it on the table. What's it doing over here?* He leaned over and noticed it was opened to the book of Ruth.

Ruth? He scratched his jaw. His Sunday school class had studied Ruth only a few months ago. *Wasn't she the gal who married Boaz? The one who. . .*

Cam gasped. He scooped the Bible into his hands and skimmed the book. Finally getting to chapter 3, he read how Naomi sent Ruth to offer herself to Boaz by uncovering his feet and lying at them.

Cam's heart beat so hard and fast he thought it would burst through his chest. The action was like a marriage proposal. It was Ruth's way of saying she was willing to be Boaz's wife. Boaz, the man several years Ruth's senior.

He drank in the slight flush on Sadie's cheeks and the sweet peace that radiated from her expression of rest. Sadie knew he couldn't have children, and yet she wanted him. She was choosing him as her kinsman-redeemer. He closed his eyes, lifting his face heavenward. *I swore I'd never allow another woman to go through what Brenda had to go through.*

"I have a plan for you and for Sadie. I know what you need."

Cam opened his eyes and gazed at Sadie. Tendrils of her long dark hair cascaded down her cheeks and neck. Her long eyelashes brushed against her ivory cheeks. She was an older version of Ellie, even in her sleep. Cam leaned forward and pushed a strand of hair away from Sadie's face. Sadie's lashes fluttered; then her eyes popped open and she bolted upright. "Is Ellie okay?"

"Ellie's fine. She's still asleep." Cam took Sadie's hand in his. "So you want me to be your kinsman-redeemer?"

A blush swept across Sadie's face, and she looked down at the floor. "Well, I—I mean. . ."

Cam pulled Sadie into his arms. His heart beat strong and loud beneath his chest, and he was sure Sadie could hear it. "I love you, Sadie."

Sadie fell into his embrace, wrapping her arms around him. A sigh escaped her lips. "I love you, too."

"You love me even though I can't have children?"

Sadie lifted her face. Cam drank in the love from her gaze. "We can always adopt."

epilogue

Eight months later

Sadie tied the cream-colored satin bow around Ellie's waist then turned her around and checked the front of the dress. She tweaked her daughter's nose. "I've never seen a prettier flower girl."

Ellie straightened her shoulders and pushed Sadie's hand away. "Mommy, I am six years old now. I'm too big to get my nose pinched."

"No matter how old you get, you'll always be my little girl." Sadie tickled Ellie's neck, making her squirm and giggle.

"Okay, girls. Let's not get all messed up before the wedding." Sadie's mom tapped Sadie's shoulder. "Stand up straight and let me make sure the buttons are all latched."

Sadie stood to her full height. She was glad her parents had flown to Delaware for the wedding. Cam had surprised Sadie by arranging for the three of them to visit her parents at Christmas. To her surprise, her parents really warmed to Cam and Ellie. She prayed her own relationship with them would mend completely one day as well.

Cam had contacted Brenda's parents about their upcoming wedding also. Though they'd only corresponded with Ellie through gifts at Christmas and birthdays, Sadie wanted them to know she wouldn't stand in the way of their forming a relationship with Ellie. It broke Sadie's heart that Ellie hadn't received a birthday present from them this year. Even more heartbreaking was that Ellie didn't even realize to miss it.

"Bend down." Her mother's voice interrupted her thoughts. "You have a flower coming loose from your hair."

Sadie looked at her mother's reflection in the mirror. Her mother was still as beautiful as she'd always been. Her hair still long, dark, and thick. Her skin still smooth and clear. Sadie hoped she would be as beautiful two and a half decades from now. Raw emotion filled Sadie's heart. She yearned for a closer relationship with this woman. "Mom, thank you for coming."

"It's your wedding. Of course we would come."

"I know. It's just..."

Her mom lightly wrapped her arms around Sadie's shoulders. "I love you, honey."

"I love you, too, Mom." Her heart swelled with thankfulness at this quick answer to prayer and the hope it raised in her.

"Mommy." Ellie grabbed Sadie's hand and tugged. "It's almost time. I saw Daddy go to the front of the church. Miss Montgomery is here, too."

Sadie's heart swelled at the mention of Ellie's kindergarten teacher. Though Sadie had once thought the woman had been responsible for spreading rumors about Sadie, she soon learned Ellie's teacher had been one of her many colleagues who enjoyed basking in God's forgiveness and redemption. The fact that Miss Montgomery was smart enough to snag up Charles Mann only made her all the more wonderful in Sadie's eyes. Sadie had never known a more contented man as the middle school assistant principal now that he had the kindergarten teacher at his side. If Sadie's guess was right, their wedding would be the next in the small community.

"Okay then." Sadie snapped from her reverie, stood, and then walked to the door. She and Cam had planned a very small wedding. Only his family, her parents, and a very few select friends would be in attendance. They had no bridesmaids or groomsmen—only Cam, Sadie, and Ellie. Sadie had never even considered a wedding after she gave birth to Ellie. Now she needed the ceremony to be intimate and only between them. She wanted to drink in the promise she and Cam would make together in the presence of God, their families and friends, and their daughter.

Her dad stood in the hall waiting for her. "You ready?" He offered his arm and winked. "You look beautiful."

Sadie felt a blush creep up her cheeks. The long, simple cream-colored dress she'd chosen fit her perfectly. The all-satin, spaghetti strap design stopped at the floor in the front with a small train in the back. It seemed to have been made especially for her. Opting not to wear a veil, instead Sadie had her hairdresser weave baby's breath and small cream roses through her hair. She couldn't wait to see Cam's face when she and her father walked through the door.

Ellie grabbed Sadie's elbow. "When's it my turn, Mommy?"

"Well, you are first." Sadie straightened the bow on Ellie's flower basket. "When the right song begins, I'll tell you to go."

Ellie twisted back and forth, allowing her skirt to flare. "We look pretty."

"You both sure do." Sadie's dad winked.

The music began, and Sadie felt her pulse race. She could hardly wait to become Mrs. Cam Reynolds. After letting out a quick breath, she nudged Ellie. "That's your song, sweetie."

❧

The doors swung open and Cam inhaled a deep breath. He'd been waiting forever for this day to arrive. His precious daughter stepped onto the white carpet. She smiled brightly at him as she dropped one petal after another onto the floor.

He glanced at his family. His mom and dad beamed at

Ellie. Kelly and her girls sat beside them, and even her oldest daughter, surprisingly, seemed happy to be there.

He noticed Charles Mann and his girlfriend sitting behind them. The sight of him almost made Cam laugh out loud. In truth, Cam should be thankful to the guy. If Charles hadn't asked Sadie out to pizza, they might still be dancing around their true feelings for each other.

Ellie finally reached the front and turned to stand beside him. He put his hand on her shoulder as the "Wedding March" sounded from the piano. "Wait till you see how pretty Mommy looks," Sadie whispered up at him.

He squeezed her shoulder. He couldn't wait. Thankfully, they'd scheduled their wedding for early in the day. He didn't know what he would have done if he'd had to wait until evening.

And then he saw her.

Her long hair was swept up on the top of her head with flowers adorning the sides. Several wisps of hair draped her neck, and he wished he could be one of them so that he could touch her softness. *Soon enough,* he thought, trying to persuade his beating heart. *She'll be all yours, soon enough.*

He drank in her dress. The spaghetti straps, though modest, exposed her shoulders and nape of her neck; and the material, so silky and shiny, draped her curves perfectly, sending Cam's mind in a tailspin.

His gaze moved up to her eyes, so full of love and hope. She and her father reached him, and he took her hands in his. "I love you," he whispered.

"Me, too," she whispered back.

In only a few minutes, Cam recited his vows. He listened intently as Sadie promised to love him, honor him, and cherish him through everything: sickness and health, riches and poverty. He devoured her sweet, sincere gaze as she spoke the words, knowing she meant them to the core of her being. Finally, he was able to kiss his bride. Her lips were soft and sweet, and once again he yearned for their time alone. He broke away, touching her cheek with the back of his hand. "Sadie Reynolds, I'm glad you found your way home."

A Letter To Our Readers

Dear Reader:

In order that we might better contribute to your reading enjoyment, we would appreciate your taking a few minutes to respond to the following questions. We welcome your comments and read each form and letter we receive. When completed, please return to the following:

Fiction Editor
Heartsong Presents
PO Box 719
Uhrichsville, Ohio 44683

1. Did you enjoy reading *Finding Home* by Jennifer Johnson?
   ❑ Very much! I would like to see more books by this author!
   ❑ Moderately. I would have enjoyed it more if

   _____

   _____

   _____

2. Are you a member of **Heartsong Presents**? ❑ Yes ❑ No
   If no, where did you purchase this book? _____

   _____

3. How would you rate, on a scale from 1 (poor) to 5 (superior), the cover design? _____

4. On a scale from 1 (poor) to 10 (superior), please rate the following elements.

   _____ Heroine   _____ Plot
   _____ Hero   _____ Inspirational theme
   _____ Setting   _____ Secondary characters

5. These characters were special because? _____

_____

_____

6. How has this book inspired your life? _____

_____

_____

7. What settings would you like to see covered in future
   Heartsong Presents books? _____

_____

_____

8. What are some inspirational themes you would like to see
   treated in future books? _____

_____

_____

9. Would you be interested in reading other **Heartsong
   Presents** titles? ❑ Yes ❑ No

10. Please check your age range:
   - ❑ Under 18
   - ❑ 18-24
   - ❑ 25-34
   - ❑ 35-45
   - ❑ 46-55
   - ❑ Over 55

Name _____

Occupation _____

Address _____

City, State, Zip _____

HOOSIER CROSSROADS

Three daughters of modern Indiana are in pursuit of fulfilling their dreams and finding peace. Kylie Andrews has risen from poverty, so she balks at Ryan Watkin's free-spirited approach to work and securing a future. Chloe Andrews is on the verge of graduating university as a star soccer player, until an injury benches her and Trevor Montgomery stands in the way of her goals. Lydia Hammond has failed at multiple jobs, but well-organized Gideon Andrews is drawn to her despite her feeling obligated to another relationship. Can romance be the tool God uses to bring these women the desires of their hearts?

Contemporary, paperback, 352 pages, 5³⁄₁₆" x 8"

Heartsong♥

Presents

Great Inspirational Romance at a Great Price!

Heartsong Presents books are inspirational romances in contemporary and historical settings, designed to give you an enjoyable, spirit-lifting reading experience. You can choose wonderfully written titles from some of today's best authors like Wanda E. Brunstetter, Mary Connealy, Susan Page Davis, Cathy Marie Hake, Joyce Livingston, and many others.

When ordering quantities less than twelve, above titles are $2.97 each.
Not all titles may be available at time of order.

HEARTSONG
PRESENTS

If you love Christian romance...

$10.99

You'll love Heartsong Presents' inspiring and faith-filled romances by today's very best Christian authors...Wanda E. Brunstetter, Mary Connealy, Susan Page Davis, Cathy Marie Hake, and Joyce Livingston, to mention a few!

When you join Heartsong Presents, you'll enjoy four brand-new, mass-market, 176-page books—two contemporary and two historical—that will build you up in your faith when you discover God's role in every relationship you read about!

Mass Market 176 Pages

Imagine...four new romances every four weeks—with men and women like you who long to meet the one God has chosen as the love of their lives...all for the low price of $10.99 postpaid.

To join, simply visit www.heartsong presents.com or complete the coupon below and mail it to the address provided.